P...
WO...

Carlo Gébler was born in ... ...te of the
National Film School, he ... ... director of films,
including *Over Here, Rati... ...man* (nominated for an
Academy Award), *Country and Irish* and *George Barker* for
the South Bank Show. He has had short stories published in
the *Literary Review*, *Fiction Magazine* and *London Tales*,
and is the author of *The Eleventh Summer* (Penguin 1986),
his first novel, and *August in July* (Penguin 1987). Carlo
Gébler lives in London.

Work and Play

by

Carlo Gébler

PENGUIN BOOKS

PENGUIN BOOKS

Published by the Penguin Group
27 Wrights Lane, London W8 5TZ, England
Viking Penguin Inc., 40 West 23rd Street, New York, New York 10010, USA
Penguin Books Australia Ltd, Ringwood, Victoria, Australia
Penguin Books Canada Ltd, 2801 John Street, Markham, Ontario, Canada L3R 1B4
Penguin Books (NZ) Ltd, 182–190 Wairau Road, Auckland 10, New Zealand

Penguin Books Ltd, Registered Offices: Harmondsworth, Middlesex, England

First published in Great Britain by Hamish Hamilton 1987
Published in Penguin Books 1988

Copyright © Carlo Gébler, 1987
All rights reserved

Printed and bound in Great Britain by
Cox & Wyman Ltd, Reading

Except in the United States of America,
this book is sold subject to the condition
that it shall not, by way of trade or otherwise,
be lent, re-sold, hired out, or otherwise circulated
without the publisher's prior consent in any form of
binding or cover other than that in which it is
published and without a similar condition
including this condition being imposed
on the subsequent purchaser

For

Pascoe Macfarlane (1945–1984)
&
Aziz Yehia (1950–1984)

'When the smack begins to flow
Then I really don't care any more
About all you Jim-Jims in this town
And everybody putting everybody else down
And all the politicians making crazy sounds
And all the dead bodies piled up in mounds'

      — Lou Reed,
       Heroin

(Written by Lou Reed. Copyright © 1966 Oakfield Avenue
Music, Ltd. Used by permission. All rights reserved.)

1

FERGUS OPENED THE cottage door and stepped outside. The blue sky was filled with low white clouds. Flat on the bottom, they were piled high on top like confections of meringue. The breeze smelt of wet grass.

He went down the steps. Through the trees he could see the lake beyond, long and grey like a cigar holder.

He circled the cottage, waving to Connie through the kitchen window, and came to the barn. The doors were held fast with breeze-blocks. As he lifted them away he reprimanded himself for not getting a proper lock fitted.

Inside there was a smell of old hay. The Morris 1000 was at the back. Strips of sunlight lay across its rounded roof. He climbed in and touched the knobbly St Christopher's medal on the dashboard, then drove away.

The road twisted from side to side. He came up behind a farmer with a herd of sheep and had to wait while they were put into a field. He passed hikers with brightly coloured knapsacks and skirted the walls of Powerscourt, catching a glimpse of old trees and rhododendron bushes through a gateway. He bought cigarettes in the village and drove on towards the dual carriage-way. Somewhere behind his navel the first trickle of adrenalin started. This always preceded his visits. Especially since the business at the start of the summer.

At the junction with the main Dublin road there had been an accident. A crumpled Ford sat by the roadside, a big sticker advertising the joys of Kilkenny in the rear window. The other vehicle, a fruit and vegetable van, straddled the central reservation. Its cargo of tomatoes had shed onto the tarmac. There were two crying boys with bleeding noses.

Fergus slipped out onto the carriageway carefully. Two miles further on he passed a garage with a sign which flashed 'open'. He began the descent towards Bray. There was a modern church and a housing estate separating him from the mountains to the south. This was the dividing line between the country and the city. The cross-over gave him a vague sense of disappointment. In half an hour he would be home.

2

The plaque on the gateway read 'Belmont'. He turned through and parked in front of the grey two-storey house. He could smell the sea and hear seagulls overhead. Everything was as always: the bed of herbs at the side, vivid green against the dark earth; the wooden wheelbarrow with the pink-petalled rose bush; the mossy sundial in the corner which his father had never cemented in place.

The front door was not locked. He went through the hall, past the table with its bronze statue of a naked woman with a gazelle which had always fascinated him as a child, and into the kitchen. A huge pan stood on the stove with dark red stains on the outside. His mother was making jam. She jumped up and kissed him on the cheeks. Her eyes were shining.

'How's father?' he asked.

'Your father's well,' she said. 'Look at this now.'

She held out a half-knitted Aran sweater to his chest. It was white and missing an arm.

'This'll keep you warm up there in the hills.'

She stared into his eyes.

'Are you happy Fergus?' she asked. 'Is there anything you want to tell me?'

2

'I'm as happy as one could hope to be.'

She ran her hand around his chin and muttered he had better go through.

'Will you take some jam home?' she asked.

He turned in the doorway.

'It's strawberry, your favourite.'

He found his way down the dark back hall, past the cupboard where they kept the crab-apples, and stopped at the door of the study. The radio was playing inside; a symphony. It would be Radio Three.

He knocked once.

'Come in, come in, whoever you are,' his father's voice sounded beyond the wood.

He went in. His father was in front of the telescope.

'Ah, it's you is it?' his father said without turning. 'I thought I heard you skulking around. Close the door.'

The hinges creaked as they closed behind him.

He looked around. The desk was strewn with papers. The black strongbox bearing the name of a London solicitor was open beside the chair. On the wall was the old nursery quoits board now used by his father for hanging all the house keys, with the face of a clown staring out from behind them.

'Have you been keeping out of mischief?'

Fergus stared at the nearly bald head of his father and his cranium which seemed to be pushing through the skin.

'Yes.'

'Still drawing the dole?'

'Yes.'

'If I got a pound for everyone of your yesses, I'd be a rich man.'

Dublin bay stretched beyond the window, Airfix grey.

'Terrible news . . . .' His father was still staring through the telescope. 'The goats are coming off the island. Young glue-sniffers have been going over at night and chasing them. They've all had a nervous breakdown, the goats I mean. I don't know what's happening to the young. Have a squint.'

Fergus brought his eye to the cylinder. At the other end danced a yacht with a red sail. The presenter announced the end of Mahler's Second Symphony.

'Why buy records?' he heard his father saying. 'When you can tape them and it's just as good.'

3

3

With a rolled towel under his arm Fergus followed his father outside. The Morris 1000 stood baking in the sun, the chrome bumper gleaming.

His mother followed with a cardboard box containing tea and sandwiches wrapped in greaseproof paper.

'This will keep the wolf from the door,' she said, and the box went on the back seat.

Inside, the car was hot, smelling of leather.

'I hope the brakes are good,' said his father fussing with the old-fashioned seat belt. They crawled out of the gate and drove down past the harbour. Small boys were fishing from the groyne with gigantic fishing rods.

'Did I tell you about the goats?' His father waved back towards the island, a long green shape with a crumbling fortress in the middle.

'You did, yes.'

'I must be getting senile.'

Fergus wound down the window. Sun sparkled on the sea in the distance. They found the Vico road and began to climb between the huge houses and the railway line.

Abruptly his father said, 'Why did you leave?'

'I don't know,' he replied. Typically, the prepared speech slipped from him and this was all he could muster. 'I didn't want to be a student any more,' he continued. 'I didn't see the point. I didn't feel I was getting anywhere.'

'What were you doing in London all last term?'

Fergus' face reddened.

'You don't want to tell me?'

'I wasn't doing anything.'

They drove on in silence. The coast curved away to the south. Blue curls of turf smoke hung in the sky.

'What have you been doing since June then?'

Fergus itemised his achievements: he had restored the Morris

4

bought from a farmer with money he had been given for his birthday despite the disgrace he was in, and he had drawn the dole. The weeks of sleeplessness and influenza, rashes, nausea and depression, he omitted to mention.

At the traffic lights where they waited to turn onto the main road, there were tinker boys with shiny hot faces. Then they motored down the coast, passing Greystones, and turned onto a dusty track. There were cars parked at the end and an ice-cream van with shooting stars painted on the side. Two women with prams re-arranged parasols over sleeping babies, while children clamoured for Mr Whippys with strawberry topping.

They climbed over the abandoned railway platform and followed the tracks along the coast. On the beach below sunbathers lay on their towels like corpses laid out in the sun. The bodies all seemed white or red: none was brown. Two girls in fringed cowboy hats were listening to a transistor. Suddenly his father stopped and put his hands on his knees as if he were about to be sick. His head shook and he started to breathe hoarsely. Fergus stepped up to him, asking what was wrong. 'The sun's making me dizzy,' his father replied.

They laid their towels on the flat sandy grass between the tracks and where the embankment sheared down to the beach. A train thundered by with faces behind the glass staring out. Faces of longing, Fergus thought. He lay back with his head on his arms and closed his eyes. He could feel the sun warming his lids and his underarms turned towards it. The railway tracks were singing. He could hear his father struggling and wheezing as he pulled on his swimming trunks underneath his towel.

'I'm going for a swim,' his father announced.

James Maguire descended the side of the embankment. The unfastened buckles of his sandals jingled as he went. The beach was shingle and he picked his way across unsteadily. He had a brown neck and very white legs with varicose veins. They reminded Fergus of knots of rubber bands.

At the edge of the sea he folded his towel and stepped out of his sandals. He went into the water with his arms held forwards. After six or seven paces he bent forward and splashed his face and shoulders. Then he plunged under the pewter surface. A moment later he bobbed up again. He swam away with his head held high out of the water. Faraway an oil tanker sailed by, like a square box resting on the surface.

Fergus lay back and looked up at the sky. It arched above him, blue, the colour of an aquarium. As a child he had often imagined that he and everyone else in the world were really inside a gigantic tank with God staring at them. He remembered this dimly and closed his eyes. His mind started to drift. Then they began, one sensation after another which together formed an abbreviated account of the early summer. The boat crossing at night from Dublin to Wales, with Tom and Connie who was Tom's girlfriend then. Euston station in the early morning with steaming tea urns dotted on the platforms. The smell of dead chrysanthemums when they first went into the room where they were to stay in Kentish Town. The snaking yellow lines laid out on the freckled mirror and the rolled-up Irish twenty-pound note which they used as a straw. The days sliding into weeks sliding into months. Connie stealing the handbag in the pub. Opening the purse from the handbag on the underground and seeing that it held a hundred pounds in cash which would get them all home and hearing Tom saying that he wasn't coming, and for the first time in his life being overcome by the sensation of remorse. The journey back to Ireland, shivering and nauseous. The letter waiting for him on the mantelpiece, which told him he'd been expelled from his course for non-attendance. Fleeing with Connie the next day to the mountains. The summer months of celibacy, restoring the car and getting himself better. His father shouting over Sunday lunch, 'No Maguire has ever failed to finish what they started.' Walking from the house, the words ringing in his ears, and driving home with his foot pressed down on the accelerator.

That argument had been in July. Now it was August and an uneasy accord had been re-established. . . .

Fergus moved from side to side, itching his back on the ground. The immediate past was a wet wound which hadn't started to heal properly and the slightest contact caused him to wince inwardly. But in time, he told himself, healing would happen and the pain would go away. . . .

4

A dog was barking loudly and there were voices clamouring.
Fergus lifted up his head and looked down. Two men were in the
water manhandling something. One wore his clothes, the other a
pair of mauve swimming trunks. The mongrel was leaping up and
down in the surf excitedly.

Fergus scrambled to his feet and started to run down the
embankment. A trickle of sweat bumped over his ribs. The
shingle was suddenly hard beneath him. Shudderings ran up the
bones of his legs. A man was being carried out of the sea. He was
white-skinned with a brown neck, mouth open, head hanging
limply. Fergus remembered the accident on the road, the pulped
tomatoes, the bleeding noses of the two boys. He saw the man
was his father.

The body was laid on the shingle and onlookers crowded
around. Fergus gave his name. The rescuer in the wet clothes
began to blow into his father's mouth. Someone threw a stone at
the dog and it scampered off whining. Fergus wanted to help.
Would that make a bad situation worse? he asked himself. Yet it
was almost unendurable, this mingling of concern and inactivity.
Then there was the question. It was swelling inside him, getting
larger and larger, until it occupied his whole thoughts. But it was
the one he would not dare to ask. Behind the blue sky he imagined
the eyes were staring without blinking.

Suddenly a huge spurt of water came out of James Maguire's
mouth. Fergus felt something inside him like a wrench. The inner
voice which had been forming the question fell silent and in its
place began another. No, thank God, said the second, it wasn't
the worst.

They carried the body up the side of the railway embankment
with Fergus following and holding his father's head. He was
gripped by the fear that because it was hanging back it was going
to fall off, roll away like a football and thud across the shingle. In
the car park the owner of the ice-cream van gave them cardboard

to put between his father and the dusty ground. Children held their Mr Whippys at arm's length and watched with wide eyes. The man in wet clothes unbuttoned his shirt and laid it over a car bonnet to dry.

It was baking hot. Fergus felt the sun on the back of his head. A smell of gelatine drifted from the ice-cream van. It had been a close call but it wasn't the last one. Then what was its purpose? Fergus wondered. Back came the reply within an instant. It had been to teach him a lesson. For a moment he imagined the eyes behind the sky widening fractionally at this. Sooner or later *it* would happen. After that nothing more could be said; no harm could be undone, no misunderstandings cleared up. That was what he had to learn. From now on he was to make the best of the little time that was left.

He looked down at his father, at his long face, at the lines that ran across his forehead, at his closed eyelids with the shape of his eyeballs behind. He felt a great rush of tenderness and joy. He would make friends with the old man. He would explain his behaviour. He would be changed. Of course his father would be changed as well. The brush with death would have softened him. As of the moment of his recovery they would start to trust each other. They would become friends.

After a while an ambulance came bumping down the track. The ambulance men were young and brisk. On the cardboard, the seawater left a stain in the shape of his father's body.

'Do you want a lift to the hospital?' one of the men asked Fergus.

'I'll drive myself,' he said. The ambulance doors were shut and it careered off down the track. Its flashing beacon seemed absurd in the bright sunlight.

'Just a turn. That's all it was,' said the man in the purple swimming trunks. He was rubbing sand off the soles of his feet.

Of course it was. Fergus had known from the first. Now here was this sixty-year-old, cleaning his feet and telling him. Fergus wanted to thank the rescuers. He also wanted them to know he had learnt from the shock and henceforth was going to be a good son. You did what you did, he wanted to tell them, now it's for me to do what I will do. But it was too difficult to explain, he thought and, even if he managed to express it, it would sound inappropriate.

8

He squeezed the hands of the rescuers and jumped into his car. He drove away very fast, hitting the ruts on the track so hard that twice his head bumped against the roof of the Morris.

5

He arrived at the hospital and they seemed to be expecting him. A nurse showed him into a room which smelt of fart and cabbage. He opened a window. On the lawn there were patients in wheelchairs.

After a couple of minutes the door opened and a doctor came in. A young man in a woollen tie. His white coat was stiff at the front.

'Good afternoon,' said the doctor.

He looked at the clipboard he was holding.

'Won't you sit down?'

Fergus said he preferred to stand. What on earth was the procrastination about? Why didn't the imbecile get on with it?

'I have to tell you . . . .'

Fergus could see the doctor was speaking to him; his lips were moving and he was clicking his pen. But surely these words weren't meant for him? What about the water which had spewed out? Daddy had almost been taken but then he had been given back. What the doctor said wasn't true. Or possible.

'I'm afraid I have to tell you your father passed away about fifteen minutes ago.'

Now at the back of his throat Fergus sensed the raw feeling that always accompanied distress and noticed that tears, warm and salty, were running down his cheeks.

'We suspect a heart attack. But until the autopsy we can't say for certain.'

His father had been half-taken. Then he had come back. Now he had been taken again. Who could have devised such a punishment? At the edge of his thoughts were the eyes behind the sky.

9

'I must ring my mother,' he heard himself saying through his tears.

He put his hand into his pocket for his wallet. The action, performed countless times, suddenly seemed weird and unnatural. From now on would everything seem so strange? Had a line been drawn across his life, separating those events before from those events which came after?

'What is it?' the doctor asked.

Fergus, rooting in his pocket, had forgotten what he was looking for. Then he remembered. It was his wallet. But his wallet wasn't there. Of course. On the beach he had slipped it for safe-keeping under the towel. His father had died, and now this. He started to wail. He could see the doctor looking at him with a startled expression.

'I don't have any money,' he said. 'I can't use the telephone.'

A nurse came and put an arm over his shoulders. She wore a label with her name, Bernie.

'I must phone my mother but I have no money.'

They led him to an office where there was a telephone and he dialled.

'Mother,' he said.

Before he could get the words out she started to cry. A faraway thought crossed his mind. It wasn't like this in stories or films. The news was delivered first and then came the reaction. Everything was skew-whiff.

He started, and when he was finished his mother cried, 'Come home,' and he put down the receiver. The nurse had brought him a cup of scalding tea and he drank it without noticing he was drinking.

6

Leaving the hospital he remembered his wallet. The idea of its being lost was unthinkable, the separation painful.

When he got back to the car park by the coast it was empty. He could see the tyre marks in the sand. He retraced his steps along the railway line. Every detail from the afternoon was before his mind's eye. The girls clustered round the transistor. The white bodies laid out like corpses in the sun. The grey Irish sea. He found the towels where they had left them. His wallet too. He grasped it like a talisman and sat down. A few feet away the mongrel was nosing in the food box. He threw a stone which hit the animal on the ribs and it ran off yelping. An oldish woman was walking by. She told him not to be cruel to dumb animals. He imagined himself replying, 'I'm sorry but I'm not feeling too good on account of my father having just died,' and looked at the woman's face. To his surprise he saw it was a rather nice face: lined, faintly tanned, red lipstick and little pearl earrings. Her eyes weren't dark and cross. They were sad and questioning. He was overcome with self-disgust at what he had imagined saying to her. 'I'm sorry,' he apologised. The woman smiled and walked away, her sensible shoes crunching the sandy earth. He called to the dog but it wouldn't come. After a while he grew tired, sat down and started to stare ahead.

Dusk was falling and the towels were faintly damp. He should go home. Mother would be waiting. Pippa too, weeping silently no doubt and rubbing her little pinched nose with balls of tissue paper. They would have telephoned his uncle Dan in London and he would be coming with his wife. Uncle Peter would probably already be on his way from North Wales, with his polished shoes and wet-down hair and tirelessly energetic manner. But he didn't want to go until he had thought it out. How was it someone could be almost taken, returned and then taken again?

He did not set off until the stars had begun to show in the sky and still he didn't know the answer.

11

7

The streets running north from St Stephen's Green were crowded. He counted four women in blouses through which the outlines of their brassières could be seen. The day was overcast.

He looked at his watch. He was early for the appointment. He bought a scotch egg and ate it in the street, getting crumbs on his chin. Then he wiped himself with a handkerchief smelling of starch. Connie had ironed it that morning along with his shirt.

Thunder was imminent. He felt weary. Since waking up that morning a faint sense of being continuously alarmed had never left him. Searching for an explanation, he told himself he was simply nervous about the coming ordeal. A life didn't simply end with a funeral, as he was learning. That was only one of the first of many full stops. Dozens more had followed: collecting his father's dry cleaning, returning his library books, cancelling a dental appointment. And each of these actions signalled, This is an end. Now there was the trip to the solicitors, and that would be another full stop. He wanted it to be over and done with and when he looked at his watch and saw it was nearly time, he was relieved and hurried along.

The office was in a modern building. In the grey paintwork of the lift someone had scratched 'IRA' which in its turn someone else had half-scratched away. The receptionist asked him to wait. He settled in a plastic chair and glanced at an evening newspaper. 'Headless corpse found near border,' ran the headline.

His mother and Pippa arrived together and they were ushered through. Mr Finnegan, the solicitor, was a large man behind a modern desk. A mock name-plate designated him as Mr Finnegan, President of the United States, complete with the American eagle. Fergus, who at other times would have thought it naïve, decided it was just a cheap gimmick.

Mr Finnegan led them to the other end of the room and they arranged themselves around a mock-Georgian table. The windows were open. The secretary appeared with teas and coaster mats. They all thanked her in turn and parrot-like she said, 'You're welcome.'

'Shall we have our tea or shall we start right away?' Mr Finnegan asked.

'I think we could start,' Fergus heard his mother saying.

Mr Finnegan fetched a brown manila file.

'Are you having a holiday this year Mrs Maguire?' he asked, settling a pair of half-moon spectacles on his nose.

'No,' she said.

Mr Finnegan cleared his throat and began to read:

' "I, James Patrick Maguire, resident in the parish of Dalkey in the county of Dublin, being of sound mind and body . . . ." '

The house in Dublin was to go to Fergus' mother and then to Pippa. Mrs Maguire was to receive money; so was Pippa. Fergus was not mentioned as a beneficiary at all.

'. . . Made this day in the county of Dublin, July 11th 198–,' concluded Mr Finnegan. 'Are there any questions?'

Nobody spoke. Mrs Maguire had her head down. Pippa was staring through the window.

Mr Finnegan muttered about copies being forwarded but Fergus paid no attention. He'd come expecting another painful full stop, another reminder of his father's absence. Instead he'd been delivered a rebuke, one that had been deliberately calculated. As the seconds passed he felt something like a swelling inside, a balloon filling up with water until it pressed all his organs outwards. It wasn't a dream. He wasn't going to wake up.

8

Fergus travelled down in the lift with his mother and sister. He stared at the dirty brown carpet on the floor.

In the street Mrs Maguire suggested the three of them went and had tea together.

'No,' said Fergus. He explained he had to meet someone and could not be late. It was a lie and he hoped it didn't show.

'Oh don't take it to heart,' said his sister suddenly; her tone was scolding.

Fergus turned and began to run. His mother and Pippa ran after him, their shoes clacking on the pavement.

'Fergus, Fergus,' they called after him in anxious pleading voices, while pedestrians looked on with embarrassed expressions.

At the top of the street he stopped, breathless. In a newsagent's, shoppers were looking at magazines with furtive expressions. He turned and peered through the streams of people moving along the pavement. Neither his mother nor Pippa were anywhere to be seen.

He found his car where he had left it by St Stephen's Green. A wizened old man was loitering nearby, leaning against the thick black railings under the overhanging trees. Fergus opened his door and the man limped over with surprising alacrity and saluted. Fergus scowled. When times were at their very worst, lunatics always seemed to seek him out. He climbed in and turned the key in the ignition. Out of the corner of his eye he could see the old man was still there, waving his arms in a grotesque parody of a policeman. The traffic was coming up from behind. Fergus wanted to drive out blindly, without looking. He imagined what would follow with an uncomfortable but acute sense of pleasure: the screech of tyres, the sickening thump of metal on metal, and the pattering of broken perspex on tarmac, the least expected yet most memorable of all accident sounds. The picture was at once terrifying and intoxicating.

'You're touching the car in front,' shouted the old man. He tapped with two fingers on the bonnet to attract Fergus' attention and gestured there was room at the back.

Fergus slammed the car into reverse and shot backwards until his bumper banged behind. The old man scurried up to the window holding out a small monkey-like little hand and said, 'Nice day your honour.'

Did he actually expect to be rewarded? Or did he want to be bought off to keep quiet?

'Oh fuck off,' shouted Fergus and drove straight out into the traffic.

Brakes squealed and horns roared. He felt exhilarated. He put his hand out of the window and made an irreverent gesture.

'Yes, and you too,' he shouted. 'You can all go to fucking blazes.'

He heard his own voice and registered his enjoyment. Be calm, he said inwardly. Hysterical euphoria is dangerous. Miscalculations are easily made. Don't get yourself into trouble. The words repeated themselves over and over.

He slowly changed up through the gears. The smell of petrol fumes drifted in. He noticed amidst the general noise that one horn was sounding repeatedly and insistently. In the rear-view mirror he saw that the car immediately behind was an enormous silver Granada. The driver was a large shape in a suit and tie, with his arm out of the window and his fingers formed into a 'V' sign. Don't, Fergus told himself. But he was just too late. The other part of him, the part that had plunged out into the traffic, had already started to react.

His hand was through the window with one finger sticking in the air and he heard himself shouting back, 'You stupid little cunt.' In the rear-view mirror he glimpsed the Granada driver shaking his fist. Fergus looked forward and smiled to himself.

The lights at Fitzwilliam Street were red. Don't look round, he said to himself. Don't provoke. Stay still. Calm was coming back. He put a cassette into the player and sat back. 'Here's to you Mrs Robinson' crackled over the speakers. He tapped on the bakelite steering wheel. He was aware of something moving by the window and his door opening. He registered that it was the burly man from the Granada. A large ringed hand took him by the collar and dragged him sideways. Two young women with brown paper shopping bags stared from the corner. Someone who was himself, who answered to his name, who spoke with his voice, was falling back towards his car with his arms outstretched. Faces were staring with anxious 'please don't ask me to get involved' expressions and the Granada driver, an ugly looking man with a large nose, was towering over him. He could feel the edge of the Morris' roof digging into his back. He'd got himself into proper trouble for which there was no one to blame but himself and now here he was, the mechanism set in motion, waiting for the worst.

A fist hit him in the face and his head sprang back, knocking

15

onto the roof. He was really seeing stars. Little silver flashes of
iridescence. There was no pain but that would come. There was
always that tiny hiatus between cause and effect. His head rolled
forward. That bastard just hit me, Fergus thought.

He pushed himself away from the car and ran forward. His
assailant was strutting away in front of him, the bottom of his
jacket swaying annoyingly from side to side. Well, he would
soon wipe the smile off his face. The man's movements told him
just what to do: a punishment suitable to the crime. He leapt in
the air while at the same time extending his right foot until he
connected with the seat of the man's trousers. The blow was so
hard Fergus was certain he could feel his shoe striking through
the flesh to the bone and for a moment it made up for everything. Sweet revenge.

The blow caught the driver unawares. He turned around
swinging at Fergus and toppled sideways, falling against some
dustbins. In turn one of these fell over and clattered along the
pavement, spilling out wadges of compounded fluff which had
come from inside a vacuum cleaner.

Fergus felt nervous. To run for it or to stand his ground? he
wondered. The man was on all fours but he was getting to his
feet. His face was dark with anger and there was fluff on his
jacket. But before Fergus had to make his mind up, two men in
blood-spattered overalls rushed out of a butcher's shop.

'Hold your horses now,' one of them said and they grabbed
the Granada driver by the arms.

It was the sort of evening-out which always came, just as
lunatics did, at times of trouble.

There was a great deal of shouting and Fergus was relieved to
see the blue serge uniform of a Gardai weaving through the
crowds towards them.

'What happened?' asked the Gardai.

'Let go of me,' said the Granada driver who gave his name as
Haverty.

The butchers released him.

'This fellow insulted me,' said Haverty gesturing toward
Fergus. 'He did this.'

Haverty held out a hand with a finger sticking up.

'I had to teach him a lesson.'

'Oh no,' Fergus replied, 'you completely misunderstood.'

16

The words had already formed. He simply had to speak them. Sometimes crises produced certainty.

Fergus turned to the Gardai. 'Mr Haverty obviously misunderstood. I was doing this,' he said.

Fergus motioned his hand as a driver would when indicating to another to pass.

Haverty closed his eyes, shook his head and shouted, 'No.'

'Mr Haverty obviously mistook my innocent gesture for an obscene one.'

Mr Haverty raised arms and then dropped them. Fergus sensed he had won the argument and for the first time he noticed the pain in his nose.

'Mr Haverty, I'm not going to do anything about you today.' It was the Gardai speaking. 'However, I'm warning you, if you carry on like this . . . .' Oh how good to hear authority issuing a rebuke.

Haverty walked away shaking his head and rubbing the knuckles of his right hand. How are the mighty fallen, Fergus thought. He sensed something indecent about his gloating. Haverty got to the side of his Granada and banged on the roof twice. Then he climbed into his seat and slammed the door with all his might. He was a child and really not the opponent Fergus had thought him to be.

'I'd get yourself seen to,' the Gardai said to Fergus. Holding his lapels he sauntered off. His jacket was too tight across his back.

'It was an unprovoked assault,' said the thin butcher. There were blackheads in his nose the size of pinheads and the colour of beetle. 'He gave you a right thump, didn't he?'

Fergus thanked the two butchers and walked towards his car holding his nose by the tip and gently moving it from side to side. The pain appeared to be seeping from the soft bone inside to the back of his face.

He slid into the Morris and shuddered with a sense of dread. It was one thing to enjoy the fearful intoxication of imagining the worst; but it was quite another, as he had done, to provoke it. He had been lucky to escape so lightly.

He waved to the butchers and moved carefully into the traffic. At Sandymount the sky went black and it started to pour with rain. It fell in thick rods and the red-and-white chimney stacks of the power station became pale fingers in the grey. It was the end

of the summer. His nose began to bleed. First it was droplets:
then it became profuse. By the time he reached the cottage his
handkerchief was dripping red.

9

It poured for the rest of the afternoon and through the early
evening. Fergus sat it out in the kitchen with water chattering in
the drainpipe over the doorway, telling Connie what had
happened and drinking tea. At ten o'clock he took his car out of
the shed and set off for the village. It had stopped raining by
then but the trees were dripping.

As he drove he stared through the small windscreen at the
dark road uncoiling in front of him. Leaves lay everywhere like
beached starfish after a storm. His nose throbbed.

In the village he parked beside the monument. A smell of
burning turf hung in the air, and in one or two of the houses he
passed he could hear the faint clatter of plates as the evening
meal was cleared away. He went into the pub. The television
was on. He exchanged a five-pound note for a handful of
change.

In the corridor outside a girl was huddled over the pay-
phone.

'No, I can't at the moment,' she said.

Then she looked quickly at Fergus and said pointedly, 'Yes,
there is.'

Ordinarily Fergus would have moved away but he was im-
patient to make his own telephone call. He leaned against the
wall as close to her as was polite.

The girl finished and made a face as she walked away. Fergus
picked up the receiver. It smelt vaguely of perspiration. He
placed his call with the operator. After a couple of moments he
was asked to put in his money. He pushed it through and heard

it dropping down onto the bed of coins underneath and the strange twanging sound that always accompanied the operation.

'You're through Enniskerry,' said the operator.

'Hello.'

'Yes,' said the voice at the other end.

'This is Fergus.'

'Fergus!' said the voice. It was Henderson. 'Where are you?'

'I'll be coming over in a week or two. Can I come and stay?'

The door of the bar swung open and laughter wafted out.

'I'll be coming for a while,' continued Fergus.

After he had finished with Henderson, Fergus telephoned a collector who he knew would be interested in buying his car and negotiated a very good price for it.

10

They drove in Henderson's frail Dyane along the M40, passing the empty space where the White City stadium had once stood.

'There she blows,' said Henderson in his mock salty-dog accent. He waved airily.

A huge council estate lay to their left. It looked like an abandoned passenger liner, with its metal-framed windows and galleries and cabin doors. Now it was clear to Fergus why he hadn't been brought to see his new home but simply presented with it as a *fait accompli*.

'You'll be able to hear the motorway traffic day and night,' said Henderson. 'Like the sea.'

Fergus muttered half-hearted words of thanks. The pre-war redbrick buildings didn't look in any way appealing. On the other hand he wasn't in a position to say he didn't like what he saw. And 'a-flat-was-a-flat-was-a-flat' as he and Henderson had chanted together when the offer had come up.

For the month up to this moment Fergus had been living with

his friend and doing odd jobs around the gallery where Henderson exhibited the works of artists, on the whole fresh from art school. In the beginning had been what they called the 'honeymoon' period. They'd drunk together; gone out together; but after three weeks they began to irritate one another. Their friendship went back many years. They both knew where the other was vulnerable; consequently, when they criticised each other, the damage inflicted was considerable. Finally, there was the size of the flat. It was on two floors but tiny. Fergus had the box-room at the back which overlooked sidings connected to the District Line. Henderson slept above and was going through his promiscuous phase. All night the trains shunted in the sidings and in the morning there were often strange girls in the kitchen. So at least there was release from all this to look forward to even if Fergus wasn't convinced of the wisdom of accepting favours from his friend.

They turned once by a bus stop black from carbon monoxide and again by a grimy public house with a garish canopy announcing 'Cocktails'. Then they turned into Natal Road and stopped at the bottom outside Mafeking House, a big five-storey block with open balconies and battleship-blue notices bolted to the walls: No Hawkers No Ballgames No Dogs. A parade of shops, several with grilles over the windows, stretched on the other side of the road. Fergus could feel gloom stealing over him, a thick, cloying sensation like the damp smell in the centre of a forest.

'I've had a few wild times here,' said Henderson.

They climbed out and Fergus took his holdall from the boot. Henderson moved towards the stairway.

There was glass in the gutter, glinting dully. The gable end of the next block was covered with graffiti. There were children playing in the space between, dark figures in the falling light. Their hoarse cries and the hollow thump of their football as it skidded about signalled winter more distinctly than the leaves turning on the chestnuts at the top of the street.

They began to climb. The steps were dark stone with silver speckles sparkling in them. Fergus heard his footfalls ringing off the glazed brick and the muted cries from the game below. His heart was sinking.

The flat was on the first floor. The door was painted a dreary ochre which was just the sort of colour Fergus thought a council would come up with. But over this it had been crudely decorated

20

with vines, olive oil pitchers and a satyr playing a set of Pan's pipes.

'Some of Kenny's early work,' said Henderson, inserting the key in the deadlock. 'He's gone more abstract now.' He turned a second key in the Yale lock.

The door opened into a hall with canvases stacked along one side. The lightbulb was dead and the air damp.

'It's only been empty a fortnight,' said Henderson, 'it'll soon warm up.'

He strode down the corridor. 'Living room in here, sir,' he said in an affected upper-class accent.

Fergus followed him in. The room was small, square and crowded with a sideboard, dining table and sofa. A long envelope stood on the table.

'That must be from Kenny,' said Henderson. 'He must have popped back. Dos and don'ts *sans* doubt.'

They stood in silence. Fergus found himself remembering the very moment his last trip to London, the fateful one, had started. He'd been sitting in one of the university cafeterias staring at his lunch. The chips were dried twigs; the beans had a scum around the edges; and the sausages were like slivers of dry turf. He had a crick in his neck from having fallen asleep in the conveyancing lecture immediately before. Rubbing his muscles, looking at his meal, he had wondered why he had bought it. What was more, why was he there? Why study law? Why hadn't he done something pleasurable like French or English? Or gone to Art School? Yes, it had been a mistake to accede to his father's wishes. As these thoughts were running through his mind, Tom had come up and said, 'Fancy a weekend in London?' Then Connie had appeared in her absurd Turkish toque and one of her velvet dresses. Her face was broad and when she smiled one of her canine teeth protruded slightly over her bottom lip. 'Coming to London with me and the boyfriend?' she asked. 'House in Kentish Town, squalid but free.' On the spot Fergus agreed. It was such an innocent first step.

'Please, this way, sir,' said Henderson, and Fergus followed.

The next room down the corridor was the bathroom, tiled and white and smelling of Harpic and with a chill in the air which Fergus connected to refrigerators. At the end of the hall, where it bent at ninety degrees, was the kitchen with apple-green units clinging to the walls. The tour ended in the bedroom which was at the bottom end of the 'L' which the flat formed. It was square with a bare bulb hanging from the ceiling. The bed in the corner sat on the floor. On the wall immediately above there was a huge mural of a female nude with pendulous breasts and thick thighs. She was sitting in a pastoral landscape filled with mountains and olive trees. A few saucers of houmous, and bouzouki music, and they could be in a kebab house, Fergus thought.

'That, sir,' Henderson had switched to an Italian accent, 'is-a-the-love-ely-Mill-ie. She is — howa do you say? — the gal-friend. Bella eh? So bootiful. Look at-a her lovely figure. She could-a show you Paradise, eh?'

Fergus had pulled back the curtains and was looking down into the yard at the back, puddles of pigeon droppings around the edges and a solitary child banging a stick onto the huge metal refuse drums. Boom, boom, boom, they sounded. He remembered Dun Loaghaire the night they left for London, the smell of diesel that hung in the air, the shouts of the dockers, and the cold as he sat on deck with Connie and Tom waiting for the ferry to pull away. Tom suggested a joint. They smoked it while a circle of envious youths stood nearby drinking from a bottle of cider. There were noises on the quayside and a rope splashed into the water. They cruised out to sea. Fergus stared back at Dublin and its lights twinkling yellow. Every time he had gone away to school, he had always stayed on deck looking back, and as the land had receded he'd got sadder and sadder. He could have gone below on these occasions but he hadn't. As he had dimly grasped, there was one part of him that wanted to be sad. Now here he was again, on his way to London and hopefully a happy time and he was doing it again. 'Coming down?' asked Tom and he followed his friends below decks and drank brandies with them in the bar.

On the train to London Connie fell asleep with her head on his shoulder, so he couldn't move. He was delighted by her touch although he pretended not to notice. Instead he stared fiercely out the window at the dreary towns of the Midlands. Nearing Euston Tom said the fun was about to start and Connie woke up and said, 'Goodee.'

The house in Kentish Town was indeed squalid. It was run by a man called Ricki. He had a mobile sound studio parked in the street outside. Within minutes of their arriving Ricki told them he wanted to make free records. 'I mean, just imagine it. Guys could walk in off the street. Anyone. They have a song, a tune. We put it down. Then someone else comes along and they really dig the record and they say, "Hey, this is really great", and we give it to them.' Ricki, who had long black hair tied up in a pony tail, steadfastly refused to look any of them in the eye. Charlatan, thought Fergus. In the afternoon he and Connie went off to the Planetarium. When they came back Tom had purchased a small deal from Ricki. Charlatan was right, said Fergus to himself. Still, whatever was on offer he wasn't refusing. He'd had it before occasionally.

They got a mirror and laid the heroin out in thin snaking lines. Fergus rolled up an Irish twenty-pound note and they snorted it up. Whatever it was cut with made the insides of their noses smart. 'It's the same as the feeling you get when you shit after an Indian,' Tom observed, to which Connie said, 'Don't be so disgusting.' Fergus felt momentarily nauseous, and then a growing feeling of stillness. The boredom of his law course became as nothing. As did his family, his father, and the tiredness he felt from not having slept the night before. In their place came a sure sense of importance. There was the universe and there was Fergus and where its axis turned, there he was. Of course it was a stupid sensation. But for a while, why not? Life was short and not sweet. So why not enjoy?

The next day Fergus cashed a cheque at a *bureau de change* and they bought another envelope. On Monday Tom said, 'Why don't we make a week of it?' At his suggestion Fergus' adrenalin began to trickle. Staying on would mean missing a week's lectures. It was dangerous. He felt as if he were staring down from a great height. He closed his eyes as if to jump and said, 'Yes.'

Boom . . . . The boy was still beating on the refuse drums. Fergus could feel his heart was beating too, pressing against his ribs.

'Once we've got the heat on it'll seem a lot nicer.'

Fergus felt Henderson touching him on the elbow.

'I know that,' he said quickly.

Henderson was looking at him closely. Could he tell what he was thinking? That he was worried? He surely looked it. Frightened too. Frightened because remembering brought him to the question. Now he was in London, did he go and see Ricki? He'd sold the Morris for quite a high figure. His mind was already beginning to take the idea seriously. No, that wouldn't do. He mustn't. This time in London wasn't going to be like the last one.

They went into the kitchen and lit the oven, leaving the door open to let out the heat. Fergus plugged in the refrigerator. When the light came on and it began to purr, he felt reassured.

They made tea and sat on stools at the formica-covered kitchen table. Fergus blew onto his drink and it steamed into his face. Without milk he noticed there were black speckles which adhered to the sides.

'Kenny used to give great parties here,' said Henderson. 'He'd make this lethal punch. His father was a chemist and Kenny said he stole pure alcohol from him for his concoctions. Probably a story but anyway, everyone used to get totally plastered.'

Fergus thought he could hear a radio playing in an adjacent flat and, more distantly, the sound of chips frying in a pan. In his mind's eye he saw his address book open at the page with the Kentish Town address. He started trying to listen to his friend. But although he could hear the words, they didn't make any sense. No, he thought, he mustn't think about it. But it wasn't to be driven off. It stayed, pressing on him like a stone in the shoe. He vaguely hoped none of this showed on his face and was relieved when Henderson put his mug down and announced he was leaving.

He followed his friend along the passage and opened the front door.

'I almost forgot,' said Henderson turning round.

He pulled out two keys from his pocket, attached to each other with a dirty piece of string, and dropped them into Fergus' palm.

'The keys of your castle.'

After Henderson left, Fergus went into the living room. He sat down on a round-backed chair. The window frames were metal, painted white. On the other side of the street he could see the shops. He heard ticking. On the shelves in the corner was a clock in the shape of the world resting on the shoulders of a silver-coloured Atlas.

He opened the white manila envelope and pulled out the letter. It was written on green-lined paper in small, rather neat writing:

Dear Fergus

Welcome to Fawlty Towers. I am very happy you have agreed to look after my flat for the next year while I am away and I am sure, as you are a friend of Henderson's, that you will treat it with respect. The good news is, all the bills have been paid, so everything from now on (gas, electricity, rates, water, rent) is down to you. I'll bill you accordingly. The bad news is, the telephone's been cut off. I paid the bill but if you want one, you'll have to pay a reconnection charge.

There's not much I can tell you about life around here. The shops are useless and the pubs on the estate aren't worth going into, even in desperation. The laundrette opposite isn't too bad but they always lose my socks. The nearest tube is Shepherd's Bush (Metropolitan line). Best place for shopping is the market which runs between Uxbridge and Goldhawk Road. When QPR are playing I tend not to go out. That's all. Drop me a line to the Fine Art Dept, University of Newcastle-upon-Tyne NE1 7RU, and let me know how you're finding things, and please look after everything, especially the canvases in the hall.

Yours ever
Kenny Ogden

Underneath, in big rounded writing was written:

P.S. Hello from Sally. (Kenny's girlfriend.) Kenny doesn't believe me but I think there's a poltergeist in the flat. I'm pretty sure he's male. His main interest seems to be in breaking the lightbulb in the hall. I think the best way to handle him is with humour and patience. (I call him Fred by the way.) If he gets up to anything, just say, 'Now Fred, you've got to stop this. I thought we were friends . . . et cetera.' Please be nice to our home and don't use the cranberry glasses (cupboard in the front room) unless it is for someone very special and adult (like your mother). It would be very nice to meet you one day.

Best wishes and goodbye,
Sally

Fergus folded the letter and put it back in the envelope. He looked out the window. Darkness had fallen and the laundrette opposite was lit up with neon. There were figures inside and drums turning. Why *had* he left the cottage in Enniskerry which had been so comfortable and quiet? He thought of Connie and the tooth protruding over her bottom lip. For a while in London they'd been occasional lovers when Tom hadn't been looking. Then they'd been fellow convalescents, living side by side in the cottage. Perhaps if he'd stayed they'd have become lovers again? He tried to think of Connie smiling but instead of her face his thoughts were filled with a fractious dialogue. It'd be safe. No. This time he'd *know* what he was doing. No. Anyway why shouldn't he? He could do what he wanted. No. Why not? Nobody cared. His father hadn't. His mother didn't. Pippa wouldn't . . . . No, he mustn't even consider it.

He jumped up and ran into the bedroom where his holdall was lying on the bed. He undid the zipper and pulled out his address book. He opened it at 'R' and there it was in the fourth box from the top: the Kentish Town address and telephone number. If he looked at it too closely he'd be lost. He ran into the kitchen. The offending page tore out easily. He twisted it back to a taper and lit the end with the flame at the back of the oven. It was burning as he stood up. Dark blue smoke curled into the air. He dropped it onto the worktop. Little charred fragments of wafer-thin paper scattered everywhere. He watched as the flames ate their way along the remaining length of white. Then suddenly they died and it was over. Fergus could still remember the address of course. It still danced before his eyes. But it no longer seemed to exercise the same effect.

He found a dustpan and brush under the sink, swept up the charred remains and put them into the swing-top bin.

11

The street had fallen quiet and he was reading *The Thirty-Nine Steps* when he heard shouting drifting up through the floor.

He raised his head feeling mildly anxious — this was always his reaction to rows overheard — and listened. He was unable to distinguish any words and it was a while before he realised the language wasn't English.

A front door banged and Fergus went to his window to look out. A man hurried along the path below and struck out across the road in the direction of the shops followed by a woman who ran with difficulty, impaired by her sari. She stopped at the kerb and called after him. The man turned and made a gesture as if he were shooing away chickens. Then he disappeared into the Kwik-Mart. The Indian woman stood for a long time on the pavement and then made her way slowly back down the path until she was out of sight.

The street was silent again. He returned to his book and read on undisturbed for the rest of his first evening in Mafeking House.

12

The following morning, Fergus came down the stairs on his way to buy some milk, and saw an Indian man wheeling a moped up the path with a dark-skinned child beside him who was clutching the moped seat.

The man was talking very angrily at the boy and Fergus wondered if he wasn't the same man he'd watched the night before.

The front door at the bottom of the stairs was ajar. Fergus stopped there, the thought idly crossing his mind that the young child might be at some sort of risk from the older man. He certainly looked terrified.

The Indians were almost level. The man looked at Fergus abruptly.

'Bloody bad,' he said. 'Hid my moped. I thought it was stolen.' Then he turned to the boy and said, 'Didn't you?'

The boy looked up. His eyes were large in the middle of his broad face.

'Didn't you?'

A faint move of the head apparently answered the man's question.

The front door folded back. Fergus saw a woman, the loops of a sari dipping from her arms. There were bracelets on her wrist. They were the couple he'd seen arguing, he decided. He noticed a smaller boy with his arms around the woman's legs.

She nodded a 'hello' to Fergus as father and child went through, and then the door shut, leaving him alone in the passageway.

13

It was dark and it was cold. He hurried down the Fulham Road and turned into the redbrick mansion block. It smelt of coffee and undefinable food smells. Nothing had changed.

He got into the tiny lift, carpet worn in the middle, and pressed the button marked '5'. The lift swayed upwards. He peered into the brass ashtray with 'Cigars' written on the front. Yes, they still filled it with sand and a few butts were poking out.

The lift stopped. He pulled back the grille doors, stepped out and carefully closed them after himself. He sniffed the air. It smelt of polish. Nothing, nothing had changed.

He went to the door with the brass '7' on the front. It was where Laura's parents lived and this evening, their third or fourth since he'd arrived in London, it was here she'd arranged to meet, rather than at the museum where she worked or a pub. He'd often visited Laura here when they were younger.

He pressed the white button and the bell clattered. He had a postcard for Laura of a Parisian shop. Shopfronts were her speciality. He took it out of his pocket. Her footfalls sounded inside. The door opened.

'Hello, hunky,' she said.

She pulled him in by his wrists and offered her face. He gave her the postcard. It showed the exterior of a nineteen-twenties confectioner's decorated with ancient gods who were eating examples of the cakes on sale. It was perfect, she said, and slipped it into her copy of *Afternoon Men* lying on the hall table.

'It's so good to see you,' she said and they hugged and touched.

He followed her into the kitchen. The red table was still there with the aluminium around the edge and the blue kitchen units and the cactus plants along the window sill. He was glad it was the same, even taking pleasure in the neon strip humming overhead.

She took a large bottle of cider from the 'fridge and they went to the living room. Laura pulled on the tasselled cords and closed the curtains. Fergus gazed at the enormous picture of the Oxford and Cambridge boats at Putney Bridge which hung over the fireplace. He remembered it from years before.

Laura sank onto the sofa beside him. Her face was oval with dark hair on either side falling straight to the shoulders. Her eyes were large and blue. Long-forgotten memories were stirring. He pictured them as brightly coloured liquids held in phials. Once the stoppers were pulled the contents turned to vapour which floated through the mind. Laura brushed her lap fastidiously and began to take tiny rapid sips from her glass. It was one of her most characteristic mannerisms. The stopper had been pulled. . . .

They were sixteen when they first met. It was at one of the dances held each term at his school. The masters who taught there — including his uncle Peter — believed it was enlightened to encourage such events. The girls came from Laura's convent.

Somewhere near the middle of the evening Laura went into the quadrangle with its red concrete floor marked into courts for badminton and huge glass roof overhead. Fergus was standing by himself. 'Can you tell me where the lavatory is?' she asked. Uncomfortable in his navy blazer and wide, coloured tie borrowed from Henderson, he led her through a maze of corridors to a door where the hand-painted sign reading 'Gentlemen' had been covered with a hand-written one saying 'Ladies'. When Laura emerged, her dress rustling, she found him waiting. He led her back to the quadrangle. Here they talked to one another and

29

enjoyed doing so. They liked each other. Then it was time to go back to the dance. But as they went in, each nervous and uncertain that what they had felt was matched by the other, they separated. Soon they lost sight of one another amidst the dancers moving under coloured lights. Now they were annoyed with themselves and set out to refind each other. It was Laura who sighted Fergus first. She went up to him and asked for a cigarette, although she had ten Sovereign in her clutch handbag. Fergus brought her down to the boiler room smelling of anthracite where they smoked in total darkness, with only the glowing ends of their cigarettes visible, and drank from the half bottle of rum which he had collected from his locker on the way there. As the bottle emptied, the stem got warmer and Fergus derived a strange pleasure from the idea of their mouths touching the same place, one after the other.

When they finished, they threw the bottle into the bushes outside where it clinked against others which already lay there, went back upstairs and slipped into the dance holding their breath in case the masters at the door smelt the alcohol. The lights dimmed and Joni Mitchell started to sing plaintively. They danced in each other's arms with their bodies touching. It was effortless and unembarrassing. Then it was Eddie and the Hotrods. They went outside and found their way to the wall which was all that remained of the air-raid shelters. They began to kiss with their lips shut. Laura's smell was a mixture of scent and something feminine which was intoxicating. Their mouths opened and they began to touch one another's tongues, furtively at first and then more boldly. Laura's teeth tasted of tobacco. Gaining in courage they clung to one another and Fergus pushed with his leg against Laura's sex.

'A Whiter Shade of Pale', by tradition the last song of every dance, sounded in the distance. Fergus walked with Laura to the car park. They wrote their addresses on each other's palms and said 'Goodbye'. The convent girls were counted and their coach set off. Fergus waved and Laura waved back, a pale figure behind rain-spattered glass. The coach turned out of the school gates and began to crawl along the road towards the village. The other boys who had come down went away but Fergus stayed, listening to the diesel engine rumbling across the dark countryside . . . .

'They're dying to see you.'

Fergus made an exaggerated mock start. With his mind drifting he had not been listening to what Laura had been saying.

'Please be your warmest.'

Laura's father, who was called Philip Shellgate, came into the drawing room first. He was wearing a velvet jacket and a turtleneck.

'How many years has it been? God, you haven't changed,' he enthused.

Ivy followed him. The second Mrs Shellgate was a small woman with a very white freckled face and red hair and a cream-coloured cossack hat resting on top of her head.

'My dear Fergus, how absolutely marvellous to see you.' She held his face with both hands as she kissed him.

'Hey, steady on,' said Laura, 'that's my ex.' Then she added: 'Phew! Stepmothers. Give them an inch, they take a mile,' and everybody laughed.

They climbed into a small car and set off. Fergus was in the back with Laura.

'All right if I smoke?' she asked.

'Oh God.' Her stepmother wound down the window. He listened to the sound of Laura inhaling and exhaling. Her body was pressed against his: one shoulder and a bony knee: all covered with the shiny material of her dress . . . .

Two days after parting in the school car park, Fergus received a bulging pink envelope, his name written on the front and Laura's name on the back. The letter inside was written on different pieces of coloured paper which smelled vaguely of scent. Different coloured pens had been used. It was signed 'lots of love' which made his heart beat. The very same morning Fergus judged she would be receiving the letter he had written. He took this to be a good omen.

After several more letters they arranged to meet one Sunday afternoon at a town between his school and her convent. He arrived first and waited as arranged by the memorial to railway workers who died in the Great War. She arrived wearing a mackintosh which was too big for her and they set off. It was a dismal day with a fine penetrating drizzle hanging in the air. All the shops were shut which made the town seem more than usually depressing. Two youths on a motorcycle kept cruising past and this made them nervous. The main hotel where they planned to have tea had a large notice hanging off the back of a chair in the hall which read, 'Tea will not be served until 3.45 pm.' When they asked if they could wait, the hotel owner told them to clear off.

For want of anything better to do they walked on, out of the commercial centre, through the redbrick terraced suburbs smelling of burnt Yorkshire pudding, and into the countryside with its sodden fields and dripping leafless trees. A car passed them on a corner, splashing their legs, and Fergus began to think it was all a dreadful mistake.

After the hotel tea of eclairs filled with cream which tasted faintly sour, they walked back to the station. A young boy had a dummy outside the ticket office and was plaintively calling, 'Penny for the Guy. Penny for the Guy.' The appeal summed up for Fergus his feelings of despondency.

'It's been more than nice,' volunteered Laura as they stood on the station platform, stamping their feet to keep warm. 'When will I see you again?'

Her words elevated what had been an afternoon of halting conversations and the discomfort of being permanently damp, into a memorable one. That evening, sitting in the study with Henderson, he told his friend that he was in love. 'I hope you know the facts of life,' Henderson replied. 'There are some accidents God doesn't forgive . . . .'

They parked in a square and climbed out. Philip Shellgate locked the doors and then made a point of checking they were locked. Ivy walked away to the edge of the King's Road.

'Do look out,' her husband shouted as she started across.

'I feel so giddy,' she called back when she jumped onto the pavement on the other side.

The restaurant was called Lily of the Valley. The purple exterior was matched by purple drapes which hung down behind the windows. Inside it was candlelit, with blue walls and seats of red velvet.

'How clever of you to find this place,' said Ivy to her husband as they settled at their table, 'and how pretty.'

'You mean unspeakably hideous,' Laura muttered in Fergus' ear.

'Awfully good moules,' said Laura's father, accepting a starched napkin from a waiter. 'Seeing as we haven't seen Fergus for a long time,' he added, 'let's have a bottle of champagne.'

Ivy rubbed her small freckled hands together and said, 'I do love you, darling.'

The wine waiter brought the green bottle to the table. The foil covering the cork came off and he began to twist the wire frame with long thin fingers. The three Shellgates stared intently, but Fergus gazed at Laura. In profile her forehead bulged in an unexpected way. The cork was coming out slowly and his thoughts were in the past . . . .

After their first meeting, Laura and Fergus saw one another almost every weekend and the following spring they arranged to spend their half-term together. Laura had the use of an empty house in a resort on the north coast of Wales.

Fergus had arrived feeling nervous. Laura kissed him but, rather than mollifying his feelings, this only made him feel worse. He asked where he was to put his things and she showed him to a room with a large double bed on which her suitcase was lying open. This was the reassurance which he needed.

They spent the evening in a cold pub called The Dragon. Fergus drank beer and Laura gin and tonic. Laura had once told him she was not a virgin and now he asked her about this. She explained that the great event had taken place in a field during a house party and she had been drunk at the time. She remembered nothing. She could not even be certain it had happened. All she knew was that when she had woken up, all her clothes were scattered around.

After the pub shut they went back to the house and drank tea. Then they went up to the room. The moon was shining through the window and Laura said they would leave the curtains open. Fergus sat down on the bed and slowly began to remove his shoes and socks. Laura undressed by the rocking chair then came and stood close to him. He finished undressing whilst she waited and they got between the cold sheets. The touch of Laura's body and her touch on him seemed utterly strange. They kissed. They became aroused. He had put the contraceptives under the pillow in advance but when he reached for them, they slipped off the end and fell down below. He had to get out of bed and feel around in the dust underneath for the flat cardboard packet.

When they were found he got back into bed, cold on his back and haunches. Laura rubbed them to warm him up. They kissed. Fumbling in the darkness, he tore open the silver foil packet and pulled out the rubbery-smelling prophylactic. He pushed the ring

33

over the end of his glans and started trying to roll it back. It did not uncurl as it had on the trial run which he'd performed in the secrecy of the school study. He remembered Henderson telling him that if it was not put on the right way it would come off during intercourse, with fatal results. He pulled it off and held it in the moonlight. He could clearly see the little reservoir on the end sticking out like a tongue. He turned it inside out, put it back on his penis and began to unroll it. This time he succeeded.

He lifted himself onto Laura and kissed her, running his hands through her hair. He noticed his finger ends were greasy and smelt of the lubricant from the Durex. He felt Laura reaching down between them and pulling him towards her and then into her. She wriggled and he pushed. There was a sensation of warmth enclosing his sex. Laura put her arms around his shoulders. He moved his hips a couple of times: then his semen trickled out in a warm, lazy way and it was over. Laura stroked his neck. 'Dear Laura,' he said. 'Dear Fergus,' she whispered. Lying in her in the darkness, Fergus wondered if there was not more to the experience but didn't ask . . . .

'Cigar, Fergus?'

Philip was pulling out a thin brown cigar that looked like a twig from the tray which the waiter was offering him.

'No thank you,' replied Fergus.

The cigar was lit and Laura's father leaned back in his seat.

'If you're from another country and you come and live here,' he said, 'you must assimilate.'

Fergus could feel Laura fidgeting beside him. They had been arguing about the position of immigrants in Britain since the main course and she'd been getting angrier and angrier. His sympathies were entirely with her.

'To integrate is simply not enough,' Laura's father continued. 'First and foremost you must become British and your sense of being West Indian or Jewish or whatever must come second.'

He had to speak loudly because the discotheque had started up on the other side of the restaurant.

'What I'm objecting to,' he continued, 'is the way we're made to feel constantly guilty about our way of life interfering with theirs. If queueing and being polite and warm beer and Sunday afternoon drives aren't to their taste, well then, they can bloody well bugger off. I'm not stopping them being British. It's them stopping me being British that I object to. Let me put it in a nut-shell for you. Everyone who goes to America becomes an American.'

'No,' interjected Laura.

'Laura, let me finish. If I emigrate to Egypt I become a bloody Egyptian. I don't remain British. That's what I'm asking and I don't think that's unfair.'

'You're frightened what we have is going to be lost,' said Laura, 'because deep down you don't believe warm beer and queueing have any real value.'

'No, I'm not frightened at all. I have absolute faith in the strength of what we have.'

'Your fear is the basis of your dislike. It's the source of your prejudice,' she replied in a rush.

'Don't be absurd, Laura. You're getting quite carried away. I don't fear or dislike anyone. I was merely trying to say I object to those who are guests in my country disapproving of how we like to live. But on the level of race or colour I have nothing against them.'

'Yeah, yeah,' said Laura, 'and some of your best friends are black.'

'Of course,' replied Philip Shellgate, 'my record there is impeccable.'

'And also let us not forget what he's done in the bank,' said Ivy. 'They employ more coloured people than all the other banks put together.'

'I know that.' Laura drew herself up.

'You can't use the National Health Service and have Social Security,' Philip began, 'unless you're prepared to say "I identify with the country which is giving me this" and that's what the immigrants won't do.'

'For Christ's sake, instead of thinking bad of them all the time, think of what they've given us.'

'Laura, you must let me finish.'

'No,' said Laura stroppily, 'you've been droning on for hours, now it's my turn.'

'What I've been saying,' said Philip, raising his voice but managing to remain cold, 'and I will repeat it — is that I resent our guests telling us that our ways of doing things are uncongenial. I'm not saying they can't have their carnivals. But

35

first and foremost they must be British.'

'But why should they?' she asked. 'Why should they become like us? Who says we should all be the same? And just think if we all were, how incredibly boring it would be. Also, you've left out the really vital question of why they've come. We conquered them. That's why they came. We needed them to work for us. Now there's not so much work around any more and we wouldn't mind if they buggered off. But it's too late for that. Finally, can't you see that this thinking that Britishness is somehow being destroyed or swamped, creates the climate in which horrible things happen and which allows the police and everyone to believe they can behave badly?'

Fergus watched Philip closely as he listened to his daughter. Mr Shellgate was pulling on his cigar and screwing up his eyes from the smoke. In between the lines on his face his skin puffed up in bulges.

'Now, Laura, you're talking real rubbish,' he said. 'I fought in a world war against fascism so please don't imply that I'm contributing to it now. My views can in no way be said to encourage what you've implied. The National Front and so on. And if you think you're going to bring me round to your way of thinking, you're going to have to do a lot better than you've been doing. Otherwise I shall take from this conversation the impression that you're still a decidedly silly schoolgirl.'

All the colour drained from his daughter's face.

'Laura,' said Ivy in her clear, ringing tones. 'You said earlier that instead of thinking badly of the immigrants we should think of what they've given us. So, tell us about that.'

'All the food, and the music, and corner shops,' she said slowly.

Fergus could hear Laura's voice was trembling. He put his hand on hers under the table.

'But it's the food mostly, I suppose,' she continued.

Ivy held her head to the side waiting for more. Philip exhaled two coils of blue smoke from his nostrils. Fergus wanted to embrace Laura. When she was hurt the effect was always the same. She seized up and couldn't speak.

'Well, we've done enough talking,' said Ivy abruptly. 'Let's dance.' She dropped her Cossack hat onto her husband's head and started to walk away. Philip raised his eyebrows lasciviously in her direction and stood up. He put the cigar in the ashtray and took off the hat.

Halfway across the restaurant, Ivy waggled her bottom from side to side and extended her arms like a belly dancer. Philip ran up from behind and took hold of her waist. As they congaed onto the dance floor an elderly couple applauded them. 'I No Cannibal' started up.

'Oh my parents,' Laura moaned.

She bent forward until her forehead was resting on the tablecloth.

'What does one do with people like that?'

Fergus rubbed the back of her hand. He considered saying, 'Shoot them,' but decided it wasn't funny.

'Let's dance,' he suggested.

She lifted up her head. A large tear had rolled down her cheek leaving a trail of wet.

'I wish my father wasn't right. I wish I wasn't such a silly girl all of the time,' she said. 'I wish just once in a while I could be grown-up and come out with grown-up arguments. I might even get my book on shopfronts written.'

They threw their napkins down and began to thread their way through the tables. The dance floor was behind a screen of greenery. Ivy gave them a little wave when they stepped onto it. She was swaying from side to side and the bottom of her skirt moved with her. Philip was shrugging up and down on the spot and gamely clicking his fingers. He took Ivy by the hand and as he began to rotate her, she beamed up at him.

'I know they're awful but sometimes they're just adorable too,' said Laura.

She put her arms around Fergus' neck and leant back.

'We should never have given one another up, you know.'

They started moving cheek to cheek. In the middle of the floor a group of young people were dancing together. The girls wore purple lipstick and lace gloves and were smoking frantically. The boys were all in narrow trousers and pointed shoes which accentuated their thin legs. Eight years before, Fergus thought, he and Laura might easily have been in place with them.

Laura sighed and lifted her head from one shoulder to the other. He remembered her standing in the moonlight in the house in North Wales, the shape of her breasts, the fuzz between her

37

legs. The music changed. They separated and started to move more quickly.

They danced on to one song after another. Fergus felt himself getting tired and then his strength coming back again. He noticed Ivy and Philip were gone from the floor. Peering past the potted plants he saw they were back at the table with their heads together like young lovers. He pointed and Laura stopped to look.

'Sweet,' she said and put her lips against his.

14

The next morning Laura woke him and told him there was someone at his front door. Far away he could hear the sound of insistent tapping.

'They'll go away,' he murmured.

Laura sighed. 'It could be an emergency,' she said and ran to the front door in his dressing gown.

'It's for you,' he heard her shouting.

He looked at his watch. It wasn't even nine o'clock and it was a Sunday morning. What did people mean by coming so early? He pulled on his clothes and went out. At the door stood a youth in an olive-green jacket.

'Sorry to disturb you. You live here?' said the youth.

'I do,' said Fergus.

'You Mr Ogden?'

The young man was speaking abnormally quietly.

'No, Mr Ogden is away for a year. I'm looking after the flat for him.'

'I see.'

The young man had his hands in the side pockets of his jacket. His short hair was very black and there were red patches on his face. He looked to his left and his right and then stared intently at Fergus.

'How are your neighbours?' he asked. 'Any trouble?'

'Everything's fine.'

The young man nodded with his mouth open.

'What about downstairs?' he asked. 'The Asians. They behaving?'

'Why do you want to know? Who are you?'

Laura was making a face.

'I'm sorry to have disturbed you. Have a nice day.'

The youth backed away from them. There was a forced smile on his face.

'Just trying to be neighbourly,' he said and disappeared down the stairs.

15

It was before nine o'clock and everyone in Oxford Street was hurrying to get to work. The predominant sounds were those of heels scuffing on paving stones and the rumble of traffic. At the pedestrian lights near Bond Street tube station he heard two women talking about hats. The green man started to flicker and he pedalled away, moving his bicycle bell continuously with his thumb to warn unwary pedestrians. Overhead the Christmas illuminations stretched across the street, showing angels blowing into trumpets. Huge, gaudy, shimmering monstrosities, they reminded him of spangled chorus girls in Las Vegas and car accessory shops that were open on Sunday mornings.

He overtook a fruit and vegetable stall with metal-rimmed wheels, tinsel wrapped around the green wooden spars, boxes of red oranges bright in the pale, wintery light, and came up behind a bus. There was a knot of passengers on the platform. They looked spruce and tight-lipped. He wondered what suburbs they had hurried from.

At Regent Street he turned right and almost immediately had

to stop to allow a torrent of pedestrians across. In the windows of a big department store young girls in stockinged feet padded about, tacking Christmas bunting in place. At Glasshouse Street he turned left and fifty yards along he turned into Golden Square. There was an old-fashioned oval-shaped post box on one side, and an old-fashioned neon sign advertising *Bennett's Cashmere House* on the other. He was there. He dismounted, locked up and went into a modern building. Jack the doorman was standing in the lobby in a suit with a woollen pullover underneath and a woollen hat on his head which he was never without. He reminded Fergus of a degenerate Punch.

'Good morning, sir,' said Jack obsequiously.

'Hello Jack, how are you today?'

'We had a fire scare,' said Jack, 'on the other side of the road. One secretary had to be evacuated. Very dishy. I always fancied being a fireman. Have you got a couple of minutes to spare, sir? I want to ask you about this crossword.'

The lift doors opened silently.

'Lunchtime,' said Fergus.

He stepped into the lift and pressed the third button.

'Goodbye, sir,' said Jack, waving with his hand from beside his thigh in a manner which Fergus found vaguely obscene.

The lift doors opened at the third floor and Fergus stepped out. Above the plate-glass doors in front of him were the words *INTERNATIONAL TELEVISION* and the logo of the company: a set of interlocking bullseyes. Inside he could see Sharon the receptionist behind her desk.

'Hello,' said Fergus.

'Oh, I feel so upset today. Really, I do,' she said. 'No, don't go away.'

'I'm not going away.'

'There's been another child murder. It was horrible. They found the poor little girl this morning.'

She sniffed and looked down at the tabloid spread out in front of her.

'It was the social worker sent to look after the little girl who did it. And what's more . . . .'

'Yes?'

'. . . The little girl's name was Sharon.'

She looked up at him. With her blonde hair, and blue eyes

and pale skin, she reminded him faintly of a hamster.

'I'll make you a coffee,' he said.

'Oh, you're a gentleman.'

He made her a cup but not one for himself and, pleading he had work to do, escaped down the corridor.

The office was at the end. He opened the heavy door and went inside. With relief he found Peter was not at his desk, hunched over the *Daily Telegraph*. Fergus closed the door and took a sandwich out of his pocket. He began to eat. It was egg with salad cream which stung the inside of his mouth. Who invented the stuff and why did the public go on eating it? he wondered. And while he was on the subject, why had he agreed to having it that morning? 'Mayonnaise, sir?' (Wide smile from the sandwich bar vendor.) 'Oh yes please.' Squidge, squidge, squidge. . . . 'That'll be eighty-five pence, sir.' 'But on the menu an egg sandwich is . . . .' (Staring at menu but not finding the item.) 'Eighty pence, you've got a good memory, sir.' (Sycophantic leer.) 'But mayonnaise is five pence extra. . . .' 'But it's not mayonnaise. It's salad cream.' 'Oh yes, sir, it is mayonnaise. Look. See, it says so on the side of the jar. *Mayonnaise, Catering Pack, 5 gallons, Contents, Emulsifier, Fat substitute, Powdered eggs, Industrial vinegar* . . . . Don't you want your change, sir?' 'Keep it. Give it to the blind.' 'Well, th . . . .' (Bangs door shut.) 'I don't know, some customers . . . .'

Fergus put his feet up on his desk. His West End Secretarial Services calendar showed a mill in Hertfordshire on a crisp frosty morning with a deep blue sky above. He shifted his gaze to the single window. Outside stretched a vista of flat roofs, metal railings and air-conditioning conduits. On a lavatory bowl abandoned by builders years before sat a seagull with its head slightly to the side. Its yellow beak was the only point of colour in the otherwise grey scene.

The night before he'd had a peculiar dream. He'd been on a rusty, creaking ferry, travelling from Dublin to Wales. The boat's cafeteria was shut and all his friends and family who were with him were hungry. He had some cucumbers and by slicing them very thinly he made enough to go round. At the end everyone was happy but himself. There were only cucumber rinds left for him to chew on.

He crumpled up the greaseproof paper which the sandwiches

had come wrapped in. Involuntarily he remembered the shingle beach, his father being carried out of the water, the yapping mongrel, and later, the oppressive, sultry afternoon in Dublin, and eating the scotch egg before going to the solicitor's. As he sometimes glumly joked with himself, like the roads of the ancient world all connecting back to Rome, all his thoughts led back to the will.

In the beginning, around the time he'd sold the Morris, he'd been simply hurt. His feelings had been, How could my father do this to me? But, once he'd accepted what had happened, he'd become angry and nursed thoughts of revenge. His feeling at this stage had been, The bastard, I'll teach him a lesson. He longed to desecrate his father's grave and to unearth some professional malpractice for which he could denounce his father. This kind of thinking had gone hand in hand with cruelty to his mother. 'You knew what Dad was doing and you encouraged it,' he had said to her on one occasion, even though he had known this was not true.

After he'd arrived in London however, there'd been a change. He began to feel he *had* done something wrong, such that he deserved to have been cut out. He could see that it was absurd and he knew he hadn't done anything that was that wrong. He'd simply abandoned his course of studies, for which his father couldn't forgive him. He could see all this but still the feeling wouldn't go away. He'd committed a crime and the eyes had meted out their impartial justice.

Now as he sat with his feet on the desk, he wondered, as he had done many times before, if he hadn't secretly wanted what had happened. If he hadn't deliberately alienated his father in order to get himself cut out because he wanted not to be happy.

As he was speculating, the door opened and Martin-Smith came in. He was an extremely tall, cadaverous man, who lived alone and played golf at weekends.

Fergus nodded a hello.

'Long time, no see, whipper-snapper.'

'You saw me yesterday,' said Fergus.

'That's what I mean,' said Martin-Smith.

Fergus pulled the large bundle of mail which was on the desk towards him. To reply personally to all letters was what he and Martin-Smith did all day. He looked at the topmost envelope. The handwriting was sloping and spikey. He decided the correspondent was old. With his International Television paper knife he slit open the top and pulled out the letter inside. It was written on lined paper torn from an exercise book. He began to read:

28, Llandudno Road
Chester Estate
Worcester

2nd June, '85

Dear Sir or Miss,

In one of your programmes you recently mentioned a figure skating champion called John Arthur Tittle. In 1962 when I was on holiday in Spain I bought a newspaper which had an article on John Arthur Tittle which I found very interesting. Until recently when I changed it by deed poll, my surname also used to be Tittle. Because of this I would like to find out more about John Arthur the skater. Can you tell me where I could do this? I have always been very interested in this man and I still have the newspaper which I bought when I was on holiday in 1962.

Thank you so very much.

'Jesus,' muttered Fergus and telephoned the Sports Department to see what information he could get on Tittle the figure skater for the man who now called himself Lilicrap.

The second letter was a request for a tee shirt with the company's logo on the front. Fergus responded with an order form which listed sizes and prices. The third was an application for a free ticket offer for a West End musical which had expired three months previously. It was from an engineer working in Saudi Arabia. He had seen the offer on a home-recorded video which his family had sent to him. His covering letter spoke of his being out of touch with the homeland. Fergus sent him a note expressing regret the offer had expired and enclosed a set of International Television beer mats.

'Blasted, bloody chair,' screamed Martin-Smith.

Fergus turned and saw the back support had come away and was lying on the floor. It looked like a question mark.

'I've asked them to get me a new one or to get this one mended so many bloody times, but does anyone bloody listen?'

Martin-Smith was on his knees trying to put the piece back in place.

Fergus opened a letter from a hairdresser in Sunderland who wanted to appear on *Science Today*. 'Once you had Mr Jones from Wales,' he read, 'talking about his new form of nail varnish remover, you accepted the principle of having ordinary people on your programme. Now it is time for myself to come to talk about Hobson's interweave system, the answer to every balding person's misery and heartache . . . .' Fergus' mind started to drift. He could feel an ache. It felt like a push behind the solar plexus and a smaller push at the back of the throat. They were old and wary friends, these feelings.

'My chair has just collapsed, I fell on the floor and I have badly damaged my back,' shouted Martin-Smith on the telephone.

16

Mid-morning, there was a timid knock at the door.

Fergus called out, 'Come in.'

'Whoever you are,' added Martin-Smith.

The door was forced back over the white shag carpet and Melanie, the runner, put her head into the room.

'There's someone to see you Fergus,' she said.

Fergus stopped typing and looked up at his calendar hanging on the wall.

'Does he have a name?'

'I think he's called something like Mr Barnes.'

Melanie was a short girl with ash coloured hair.

'What does he look like?' He remembered that when Martin-Smith last shouted at her, Melanie had burst into tears.

'Like any man. Like Jack downstairs.'

That was no recommendation. Melanie nervously rotated the gold chain around her neck.

'Go and tell Mr Barnes or whatever he's called I'm not here. Tell him I've gone out and I might not be back for the rest of the day.'

'I can't do that. Sharon said you were here.'

'Sharon told him I was here?'

'Yes, Fergus. He's sitting in reception with her.'

Fergus went into the corridor and started to stamp towards reception.

'I've got a job for you,' he heard Martin-Smith saying to Melanie behind him. 'My chair's broken and I want it fixed. Today. Comprendo?'

Awards won by the company's television programmes hung in frames on the walls.

'Look at that little girl who's just been murdered by her social worker,' he heard Sharon saying at the corridor's end. 'She was called Sharon.'

Fergus shot into reception and collided with the chesterfield hidden behind the corner.

'You're going to do yourself a serious injury if you don't watch out,' said Sharon.

Fergus rubbed his leg above the knee.

'This is Mr Wiggins,' she continued.

The figure on the second sofa was rising to his feet.

'You must be Mr Maguire,' he said.

'Yes I am.'

'What a pleasure to meet you, sir. My name is Wiggins.'

The man extended a large fleshy hand.

They settled on the leather chesterfields opposite one another. On the table was a square jug filled with flowers.

'Can't see you for the vegetation,' said Mr Wiggins. 'Do you mind?'

Mr Wiggins slid the jug away and Fergus found himself looking at a man in his fifties. His skin was shiny as if he had only recently shaved. His most prominent feature was his nose which was very large. There were black hairs sticking out of his nostrils, wiry like the legs of insects.

'I hope you don't mind my barging in like this?'

'What can we do for you?' Fergus repeated.

'I sent you my book, some months ago in fact. I received a reply, acknowledging receipt, but I haven't heard anything since.

45

It was called *The Torture Papers* and subtitled 'Acts by the State Against a Private Person'. I've sent a copy to every member of Parliament, all the members of the CBI and leading churchmen. So far the response has been very encouraging. Yes. I must say I'm very encouraged.' Mr Wiggins quickly looked from side to side and added, 'There are still pockets of freedom in the midst of dictatorship.'

'Your book,' said Fergus in an especially mild voice, 'did I reply to you about it?'

No, not you. One of the agents. A man called Martin-Smith I think. I could tell he was one of them from the way he signed himself. There was a certain wiggle to his writing.'

'Why did you ask for me then?'

'When I came in here I talked to the young girl.' He pointed towards Sharon and then leaned forward. 'You've got to be careful of young girls,' he whispered confidentially, 'but I think this one's all right. They're not usually interested in lower-class ones like her. I asked her who was the most sympathetic member of your public response department. She gave me your name.'

'You've explained the situation very clearly,' said Fergus. 'But I'm afraid I can't do anything about the matter myself as the ball's in Mr Martin-Smith's court and it wouldn't be right for me to infringe on his area. Now I'm afraid time is pressing and if you'll excuse me, I really must get back to work. I have a pile about this high on my desk.'

'Have you seen my book?' Mr Wiggins released the catches on his briefcase and lifted the lid. Inside there were three dozen identical paperbacks. Mr Wiggins took one out, blew on it, and handed it across.

'I'll make you a present of it.'

'No, I really can't accept,' said Fergus.

Mr Wiggins put the book down in front of him. The title, *The Torture Papers*, was printed in red on a white background.

'Thank you,' said Fergus, 'I shall read it with great interest.'

He stood up.

'Do you know your way down?' he asked.

'I know when it's time to go,' said Mr Wiggins flushing red. 'Everyone treats me as if I was mad but I'm not mad. No sir, not mad, not mad.'

46

Mr Wiggins smiled sadly and a moment later had disappeared through the door.

'What a nice man,' said Sharon.

Fergus said, 'Never ever give people my name, or call me out to meet them without warning. It's company policy.'

'What is?'

'We are not meant to deal directly with just any person who walks off the street. That man could have been a bomber or a killer or a lunatic.'

'All right, all right,' said Sharon, 'I just thought he was nice. I won't do it again. Coffee?'

'I suppose so.'

'I'm very good to you, Fergus Maguire. I look after you, and don't you forget that.'

As he walked down the corridor, Fergus opened *The Torture Papers*. On the first page there was a paragraph headed 'Printing History'. Fergus read:

Charlie Wiggins, the author of this book, could find no printer whom he could trust with his manuscript. Too often in the past, crusaders against the dictatorship have had their work destroyed by secret employees of the state working in printing shops. Therefore, in order to bring this work before the public, the author, Daniel Wiggins, had to master the art of printing himself. This text was printed and bound by himself with his own hands, in his own house. Like-minded citizens who wish to answer his clarion call are urged to master all means of production or, if more convenient, to seize them. This is the only way to stop the means of production being used against us.

Fergus opened the door of his office and stepped inside.

'Do you have any recollection of this?'

He dropped *The Torture Papers* onto Martin-Smith's desk. His colleague did not look up. Fergus regarded the side of the older man's face and the file of paper on which he was composing a reply in his neat, fastidious writing.

'You're too noisy in the morning,' Martin-Smith said. 'You must learn to control your surplus energy.'

'Please answer my question.'

47

With the end of his pen, Martin-Smith turned the book.

'I don't think much of the title.'

'He was outside just now.'

'Oh don't whine,' said Martin-Smith. 'It's very unbecoming.'

'You haven't been dealing with a madman like I have,' said Fergus. 'I have every right to whine.'

17

It was getting dark when Fergus pedalled into Natal Road, and the sodium street lights were on, casting their sickly yellow glow. Three youths were standing outside the fish and chip shop. With forked plastic sticks they were spearing their chips. Behind the glass he could see Mario in his white coat washing down the formica tables.

He lifted the bicycle onto the pavement and walked towards his stairs. There was someone sitting at the bottom, huddled in the gloom. Not until he was close did he see it was Mrs Singh, the woman who lived in the flat underneath.

'Hello,' he said, 'what are you doing?'

She stared with her small, brown eyes which always reminded him of a chihuahua and made a face. Her two boys were sitting on the stairs beside her.

'Locked out?'

Mrs Singh moved her mouth, turning it down at the edges.

'Where's Mr Singh?' asked Fergus.

Mrs Singh raised her arms and dropped them. 'He has gone to work,' she said slowly. Beyond her dark made-up lips Fergus could see her broad pink tongue working as she spoke.

'When does he come back?' Fergus wheeled his bicycle towards them and the two Singh boys cowered closer to their mother.

Mrs Singh gestured again, this time with her shoulder. She had an extensive vocabulary of such movements.

48

'I don't know. When the restaurant closes.'

'Does anyone have a key?'

'Only my husband.'

He put his bicycle away and fetched Kenny's plastic toolbox. In the middle of the Singhs' door there was a fireproof pane of glass. It was the same as every door in the block. He took away the slats, tacks and putty which held it in place and the glass fell forward.

'Voilà. Behold the hole,' he said.

'But what happens when my husband comes back and sees this?'

She was looking at him nervously. He felt mildly annoyed. Obviously he wasn't going to leave it like that.

He reached through, found the latch and tugged. The door swung back.

The two boys jumped up from the stairs. Brown-skinned, dark-haired, both with arms and legs like rods inside their clothes. Ravi was nine. His brother was seven.

'Go to the bedroom,' said their mother awkwardly.

Ravi, who had been holding the tacks, dropped them into Fergus' palm and the boys scuttled away.

'You've been very helpful,' said Mrs Singh.

He put the glass back and hammered in the tacks. On the stairs Mrs Singh hummed with false enthusiasm. Inside he could hear the boys running and laughing.

'You come from London?'

'Ireland.'

'You come from Ireland?' repeated Mrs Singh. 'Yes. You told me before.' He had told her before during one of their conversations on the stairs. Of his neighbours she was the one he probably knew best.

'It is a very green place?'

'Yes.'

'Not the same as where I come from.'

'I don't know. Where's that?'

'Calcutta.'

'Not a green place.'

'No. Not a green place.'

He picked up the wooden slats and saw Mrs Singh tugging on her earrings nervously. She smiled weakly.

'Any chance Mr Singh might come back for something?'

49

She shook her head brusquely and he began to knock the slats into place.

'There are no snakes in Ireland,' Mrs Singh stated.

'No.'

'Saint Patrick banished them,' she said.

'So they say.'

'Ravi, my eldest, he did a project on Saint Patrick at school.'

'There are no snakes in Ireland because of the Ice Age,' he replied.

'Maybe, you would know best.'

'Then again, maybe Saint Patrick really did banish them.'

'Yes, maybe. You would know best. Can I ask you about something?'

'Of course, Mrs Singh.'

She went into her kitchen and came out with a piece of paper, shutting the kitchen door after herself. The fourth slat slipped into place.

'Can you tell me what this is?'

'St Joseph's Sports Programme,' he read at the top. She ran a fingernail along the words 'Second XI'.

'What is this? Second XI?'

'It's to do with the teams for football. Football the game. It means the second football team. The second eleven. X and I mean eleven.'

He picked up his toolbox. 'Lucky I had the tools.'

'It was lucky.'

He went up the stone stairs. From one of the balconies above he could hear someone shouting, 'Don't forget the Fairy Liquid.' He looked over the parapet and saw a thirteen-year-old girl in a pink dress, running across the street with a purse in her hand.

The front door of the flat clicked behind him. He put the toolbox in the front room, went to the kitchen and turned on the kettle. Then he thought, Mrs Singh didn't say thank you.

At that moment he heard a timid knock at the front door. He went back and opened it. It was Ravi. In the gathering dusk his dark black hair seemed inky blue. He was wearing brown flared trousers and a brown shirt with a huge collar.

He pressed a tin into Fergus' hand.

'What's this?'

'From my mother.'

'Who was Saint Patrick?'

Ravi stared at him. 'He banished the snakes, didn't he?'

Fergus smiled and waved his hand. Ravi turned and ran. Closing his door Fergus looked at the tin and saw it contained lychees. The top was speckled green with age.

Suddenly the lightbulb in the hall exploded and splinters of glass pattered down. For a moment his heart raced in the dark, then started to slow down when he realised what had happened. He crunched across the shards to the kitchen, returning with a dustpan and brush.

After the slivers were swept he went into the front room and looked out. The girl in the dress was carrying a bag of shopping back from the direction of the Kwik-Mart. In the laundrette the attendant, Mrs Walsh, was piling wet clothes into a spinning tub.

'All right Fred,' he said out loud, speaking in the direction of the hall, 'if we're going to get on we can't have any more breaking lightbulbs.'

18

'Are you going to the party?' Henderson asked.

'No, I don't even know the girl who's giving it,' said Fergus.

They were sitting in the bar of the Sacred Heart, where Henderson often drank after he closed his gallery around the corner. Fergus looked round the room. There were a few after-work drinkers. The tables were solid oak, smelling of wax, and huge vases of flowers stood on gargoyle heads. At the official opening a chorus of choirboys had sung behind the bar. There was a photograph to prove it.

Henderson caught Fergus' eye and waved towards the corner where the two girls who served and an older man were doing the *Times* crossword.

'Do you know the manager, Bertie?' he asked.

Bertie was in his fifties with thinning hair and a pair of spectacles hanging by a chain around his neck.

'Bertie writes poetry,' said Henderson. Then he went on, 'Where did you hear about the party?'

Oh Christ. Not again. 'I don't remember,' said Fergus wearily. 'I think it was Laura who said something about it. Does he write good poetry?'

'I don't know, I haven't read any.' Henderson took the paper clip from the top of the menu and started to open it out. 'Tell me,' he continued, 'how is Laura?'

'Well enough.'

'Do you see much of her?'

'From time to time. She's a friend.'

'She's quite a girl.'

'I suppose we'd better have another drink,' said Fergus.

'Yes,' said Henderson, 'I suppose we ought.'

He drained the dregs from his glass and picked up the price list. 'What are we going to have?' he asked. 'Another kir or shall we change?'

'I think I just want plain white wine.'

'I think I'll join you. Can you get one of the waitresses? You're prettier than I am.'

Fergus waved unenthusiastically towards the corner. Henderson was tight, and he could see what was coming. He got the waitress; he ordered the wine; and then at the end of the evening he would get the tab because it would have been assumed he was the host and Henderson would say, 'Thank you very much,' as if it had been agreed from the start that Fergus was doing the treating.

After a few moments of waving which failed to get any attention, he turned back to Henderson and said, 'They don't seem to be paying attention.'

'You'll probably have to go over,' said Henderson.

At that moment Laura came through the door wearing a man's tweed coat and a tartan scarf.

'Terrific,' said Henderson. 'It's your old flame. Didn't you say she told you about the party?'

'I think so.'

'Maybe she'll get us in.' Henderson waved her over.

'Hello boys,' said Laura. 'Fancy meeting you here.' She pushed

52

the beret she had been wearing into her pocket and pulled off her scarf.

'Are you going to the party?' asked Henderson.

'What party, darling? I go to so many.'

At that moment the blonde waitress appeared.

'We'd like some drinks,' said Fergus. 'A bottle of house white and what would you like Laura?'

'*Rien*. I'm with Alfred.' She waved towards the door. 'He's parking the car.'

The blonde waitress said, 'A bottle of house white then?'

'And don't forget the ice bucket,' Laura called after her. It wasn't rude but it wasn't polite either. Suddenly Fergus had the vaguest of vague intimations the evening could be heading for calamity and then Henderson said, 'Are you going to get us into the Dixons' party, Laura?' and the feeling vanished like a silver fish going under a rock.

Laura, who had been standing with her arm draped over Henderson's shoulder, stepped away, unbuttoned the front of her coat and pulled it wide open.

'Do you think my tits are too small?' she asked.

'No,' said Henderson staring at her chest, 'I think they're very nice.'

'I know they're very nice but are they too small? My sister said so last night.'

'How is your sister?' said Henderson. 'She's almost as lovely as you are.'

'I'm not speaking to her at the moment. Not since she started casting aspersions on my body beautiful.'

'Are you ever going to grow up?' asked Fergus.

Laura stuck out her tongue at him. Small, pointed, and pink, it reminded him of strawberry ice cream projecting from a cone.

'Evidently not,' he said.

An enormous man in a crumpled suit appeared at Laura's side.

'This is Alfred. He's from America. He's going to help me with my book. Aren't you, Alfred? Going to find me a publisher?'

'I hope so,' said Alfred.

Fergus stood up and shook the huge man by the hand. His grip was rather weak. Henderson stayed where he was and nodded at the American.

'Are you on holiday?' asked Fergus.

53

'Sort of work and play combined,' replied Alfred, 'the way you Britons love to live.'

'What sort of work?' asked Henderson.

'I'm writing something about the City: attitudes to new technology; comparing it with Wall Street.'

The blonde waitress returned with a bottle and two glasses. She had a sour, down-turned mouth, Fergus noticed.

'Bye-bye, boys,' Laura said, running her hands through Henderson's thick hair.

Alfred said, 'It's been very nice meeting you. Maybe catch you both later.'

Fergus watched Alfred and Laura going to the bar. She let the American help her onto a stool and crossed her legs. In the mirror behind the bottles she saw Fergus looking, smiled and gave him a little wave. Then she turned to Alfred and began to talk in earnest to him.

Henderson said, 'I do like Laura.'

'So I gathered,' said Fergus. 'You like her a lot.'

'Do you think she'll get us into the party? She's being awfully coy about it but I'm sure she's going. I think she knows Sophie Dixon or whatever she's called.'

'I don't know. I have no idea.'

'I really feel like a party,' said Henderson. 'I really feel in the mood.'

He began to move flakes of ash that had fallen on the table from his cigarette with the tips of his fingers.

'I wonder if anyone else is coming in?'

The manager wandered up. 'Everything all right?' he asked. The spectacles were swinging around his neck.

'Hunky-dory,' replied Henderson. 'Do you know Fergus Maguire?'

'Your face is familiar,' said Bertie to Fergus, giving him a half-hearted look.

'I come in here quite often,' said Fergus.

'Any idea of the Test score?'

'No idea,' said Henderson. Fergus shook his head.

Bertie said, 'My bollocksing battery's flat, otherwise I'd go and listen to it in the car. See what tricks the Indians are up to. The AA have kept me waiting two hours. It's so demoralising.'

'Why don't you call that number that gives the scores?'

54

suggested Henderson.

'Yes, why don't I? Why don't I try that?'

The telephone began to ring. Bertie raised his eyes upwards.

'I don't know about you but I'm absolutely bloody exhausted,' he said.

He sauntered over to the telephone and picked it up.

'I'm sorry,' he boomed, 'we're absolutely solid tonight.'

He dropped the telephone on the cradle and turned back to them. 'Half past six and they expect to get a table. Morons.'

Two girls appeared in the doorway, muffled in coats and gloves.

Henderson said, 'It's Hetty and Jennifer. Things are looking up.'

'Hello,' said Bertie as they stepped onto the huge mat with 'Welcome' on it which lay across the threshold. 'Any idea what the latest cricket score is?'

The girl who was called Jennifer opened the string bag which was hanging over her shoulder and rummaged around in it for a moment or two. Then she looked up and said, 'I'm sorry, I thought I had a *Standard* but I don't,' and the bag went back on her shoulder.

Jennifer and Hetty came over and kissed Henderson on the cheek in turn.

'Do you know my friend McGillycuddy of the Reeks?'

Fergus stood up and said, 'We've met before, I think,' referring to the times Jennifer and Hetty had been in Henderson's flat. If he wasn't mistaken they'd each spent the night with his friend.

'Oh yes,' said Jennifer, smiling palely. Hetty remained blank and expressionless. Can't like me, thought Fergus and shook her hand very hard until she said, 'Ow,' and had to withdraw. 'I'm called Fergus,' he added jovially.

'Have a drink with us,' Henderson said. 'Laura's in,' he added, waving in her direction, but neither Jennifer nor Hetty seemed particularly interested. They hung up their coats on the rack by the door and settled down. The blonde waitress brought over two more glasses.

'Thanks,' said Fergus but the sour mouth didn't move at the edges.

Hetty said, 'Do you like my new shoes?'

She lifted her leg onto the table. Her shoes were black pumps with little red bows.

55

'Aren't they nice? Jennifer gave them to me. Wasn't that generous of her? You're such a generous girl Jennifer.'

'What was wrong with them?' asked Fergus.

'You used to go out with Laura, didn't you?' replied Jennifer, ignoring his question.

'That was ages ago,' he said. 'When we were at school. Her convent used to come to our dances.'

'She said you were a "broth of a boy".'

'What is that meant to mean?' interrupted Henderson. He was filling the glasses.

'It's an Irish expression. It means health and liveliness and living life to the full.'

Hetty said, 'Does it mean you're good in bed?'

Jennifer said, 'Do you live in a huge crumbling house in the middle of a vast estate?'

'The family house is in a Dublin suburb,' said Fergus, 'and it was built in the twenties. It has four bedrooms. Does that count?'

'What a pity. I was rather hoping you were an Irish baron.'

She looked across the table and smiled archly at Fergus. She had a round elfin face, sticking-out ears and brown eyes. Her most prominent feature was her large freckles. He rather liked the look of her and smiled back. Then he looked over her shoulder and saw Laura coming towards them.

'Hi gang.'

Jennifer and Hetty greeted her in unison.

'My tits really are too small,' said Laura, looking at herself in the mirror above the seats.

'Oh stop drawing attention to yourself,' snapped Hetty, 'and sit down.'

'That was incredibly hurtful, Hetty,' said Laura, pretending to sniff tearfully, 'and quite unnecessary.' She accented each of the words for a truly tragic emphasis. 'If I reveal my deepest fears in public, the least I would expect is that my oldest girl-friend support me. I think I'm going to cry. . . .'

Henderson was holding Laura by the waist. 'Why don't you tell me your deepest fears?' he said.

'I couldn't do that,' said Laura. 'You're a man. And what are all men, girls?'

'It's the "c" word,' said Laura and Hetty together.

'Mind you,' Laura added, 'I do love a cunt. They're irresistible. Who wants a man that's nice?'

'You really are very beautiful,' said Henderson.

Laura said, 'I know.'

'Where's the gorilla?' Henderson asked.

'Gone to the men's,' said Laura, 'to powder his nose.'

She held a finger to her nostril and inhaled deeply. 'That's cocaine you know, Fergus.' Then she turned to the others and said, 'Poor boy. From across the water. Complete innocent you see.'

Everyone laughed and Laura smiled at him. He remembered his father, after he'd first met her, describing Laura as a 'card'. The phrase had never left him.

'Do you think the gorilla will powder our noses?' asked Henderson.

'He'll certainly powder mine, darlings. And can we please desist from calling him the gorilla? He's a publishing contact and he has a name.'

Alfred reappeared at the top of the stairs which led up from the lavatories. Laura sprang to her feet and said, 'We're thinking of eating. Anyone hungry?'

'I wouldn't mind a bite,' said Henderson.

'I'm counting on you girls. I don't want to eat alone with Alfred. Woman's intuition tells me he's going to pounce.'

She squeezed Hetty by the neck until her friend started to squeal.

Laura went back to the bar and settled on her stool. Her dress buttoned at the back and there was a dark mole on her right shoulder blade. Alfred came up beside her with his hand in his pocket, took something out and handed it to her.

'Not exactly subtle,' said Henderson.

Laura climbed down from her stool and began to mince towards the stairs.

'See you laters, alligators,' she called over her shoulder.

Henderson and Hetty began to talk. Fergus looked at Jennifer and raised his eyebrows. Yes, she was nice. He liked her face with its freckles, her hair, her slightly plump arms. He could feel a faint stirring behind his stomach which he hadn't felt for a long time.

Jennifer said, 'I won't ask the obvious question. I won't ask what you do.'

57

'You can,' said Fergus, 'but it's not very exciting.'

They started to talk — though not about work — about his bicycle and the flat and the family of Indians who lived underneath, until Laura appeared again and did a little skip by the side of the table.

'What did you think of my Irish jig, Fergus?'

'Very good, you could be all-Ireland champion.'

'Any more thoughts on dinner? I'm counting on you all to help me preserve my honour.'

'Is he that bad?' asked Hetty.

'No, he's sweet really. He's just incredibly boring.'

'I'm game,' said Henderson.

'We might not get a table,' said Fergus. 'I think they could be all booked up.'

Henderson twisted round in his seat. 'Bertie,' he called over to the manager behind the bar. 'Any chance of a table for six?'

'We're absolutely solid,' said Bertie, 'and I should say no. But seeing as I know you, we'll fit you in. Tell the girl upstairs to give you table four.'

Alfred, who was standing a little away from the table, tugged at the crumpled front of his linen jacket.

'He's spifflicated,' whispered Laura.

Fergus said, 'Lower your voice Laura. He can hear you.'

She stared at him with widened eyes. 'Just because we used to go out together doesn't mean you can tell me what to do, darling.'

They started to climb the stairs in a ragged bunch. On the walls were photographs of famous patrons, many of them autographed. The dining room at the top was large and blue with a vaulted ceiling and a skylight above. Fergus thought it was not unlike a small chapel, except it was filled with tables and chairs. They were shown to a corner by the same blonde waitress who had served them downstairs. She brought them a basket of bread. A large painting of three girls in Edwardian dresses hung on the wall above the table.

'What are they doing?' asked Laura as she sat down.

Alfred said, 'It looks like they're flying a kite.'

'Yes, they are,' said Henderson.

Hetty said, 'The place is practically empty.'

They all looked around. There was one table close by with a

party of six presided over by a man with a moustache and two occupied tables at the other end: one with a couple holding hands, and the other with a foursome who had silver photographer's cases under their chairs. The other fourteen or so tables were unoccupied.

Fergus said, 'I thought this place was meant to be packed. Didn't we hear the manager turning people away earlier?'

Henderson broke open a piece of bread, scattering crumbs all over the tablecloth.

'Bertie turns away half the people who ring up out of sheer laziness,' he said.

'You mean the guy who runs the restaurant doesn't want people to come eat here?' asked Alfred.

'Correct.'

'Wow, England's weirder than I thought,' said the American. 'No wonder the country's going bankrupt.'

'Yes,' said Henderson. 'We're so weird we don't have the death penalty or your record of race relations but we're hoping to import them and then we'll be normal.'

'I wish you luck,' said Alfred.

'I didn't realise they had kites in Edwardian times,' said Laura. She had been gazing at the picture all the time.

'Of course they did,' said Fergus, 'and the Chinese were flying them a thousand years before.' As soon as he finished he felt rather embarrassed and made a mental note to keep quiet for a few moments.

The blonde waitress came over to take their orders. Hetty and Jennifer ordered starters as a main course. Fergus and Henderson ordered a main course but no starters. Alfred ordered a starter and a main course but asked for them to be brought together so no one would be held up.

'What about you?' said the waitress turning finally to Laura.

'I'll have a side salad.'

'The side salads are very small,' said the waitress.

Laura's hands flapped at the ends of her wrists as she considered this.

'Have you noticed how junkies do that?' said Henderson to Fergus, imitating Laura with a limp-wristed gesture. 'Except she's not a junkie of course,' he added.

'I'll have a salad niçoise then,' ordered Laura.

Fergus said, 'William Burroughs describes the puppet hands, doesn't he?'

'Do you like William Burroughs?' asked Jennifer.

Fergus said, 'I've only read one book,' and re-vowed to keep quiet.

The waitress slipped off. Laura made a face. 'I don't think that waitress likes us,' she said.

'Stupid bad-tempered old cow,' muttered Hetty.

There it was again, he thought. Hello disaster, come over here and give us a hard time. He looked across the table at Jennifer and attempted to spear a piece of frozen butter with a breadstick. Somewhere at the back of his thoughts flickered the old image of the eyes, gazing down on him and the others, just as they had on the beach.

The wine arrived. When her glass was filled Laura picked it up.

'God, I'm not even a tiny bit drunk yet,' she said.

'Oh, really. I feel as though the room is spinning around,' said Alfred. He held his head with both his hands.

'Breathe deeply,' ordered Jennifer.

Laura took a long drink of wine and wiped her lips.

'The night's young. I can still get blotto,' she said.

Henderson said, 'How's the job, Jennifer?'

'Oh don't ask me, it's a nightmare.'

'What do you do?' asked Fergus. 'I never did get a chance to ask you.'

'I work for a small publishing company.'

'Any that I would have heard of?'

'Arthur Books.'

He had heard of them. One of their bestsellers had been a photographic guide to the nudist beaches of Europe called *Bare Essentials*. It had been presented to a departing accountant at the end of Fergus's second week at work. Even though he was new he'd signed it. He'd had to. Sharon insisted, pressing the pen into his hand and saying mysteriously, 'You can't beat us so you've got to join us.'

Jennifer said, 'I work on the women's imprint. It's not too bad really. It's just that I don't want to see another book on natural childbirth for the rest of my life, and I can't stand the girl above me. Do you know Amanda Hardcastle?'

'Yes,' said Henderson.

Fergus had never heard of her.

'We call her Amanda the Hun.'

'That's a bit rough,' said Henderson. 'I think she's sweet.'

'Oh no she's not. She treats me like a skivvy. She won't speak to me but leaves me notes on the stairs. "Jenny do this. Jenny do that." I'm sure she calls me Jenny because she knows I hate it. Sometimes she even spells my name with an 'i' just to annoy. You know, J-E-N-N-I. Last week she called me into her office and asked me to do up her suspenders before she went out with her boyfriend. I think she's a power-monger.'

The blonde waitress carrying plates arrived and said, 'Lamb chops?'

Fergus put up his hand.

'Salad niçoise?'

'Oh mine,' said Laura.

It was served in a large wooden bowl.

A waiter brought Alfred his field mushrooms smelling of herbs along with his enormous steak on a separate plate and Hetty her crudités. As soon as the dish was in front of her she dipped a stem of cauliflower into the curry sauce and noisily chewed off the head.

The blonde waitress returned with the two final orders. Henderson indicated that his was the moussaka before she could ask, and so the plate of potted shrimps went in front of Jennifer.

Fergus glanced down. He was hungry and each of his chops was about the size of a postage stamp. He looked around. The other portions were similarly tiny. A memory of the exorbitant figures on the menu briefly returned. So this was eating out?

Laura said, 'I'm afraid my salad niçoise isn't quite right.'

Fergus began to lift haricots verts from the plate which the blonde waitress was offering him.

'The chef made it for you specially,' she said.

'I'm afraid the egg's too hard,' said Laura.

'Be quiet Laura,' said Hetty.

Fergus had taken two spoons of butter-free green beans; now the question was, did he take two or three potatoes from the other half of the vegetable dish?

'I can take it back for you if you like,' said the blonde waitress coldly.

Laura was holding half an egg on the end of her fork. The

61

white was glazed and shiny. 'A salad niçoise egg should always be slightly soft so you can mix it in,' she said.

Fergus decided to take the two biggest potatoes. Two was less than three yet there was probably more bulk in them.

'I'll deal with it,' said the waitress.

'I don't like to make a fuss . . . .'

The waitress set down the vegetables, picked up Laura's plate and was gone before she could finish her sentence.

Everyone began to eat. Hetty looked across the table. 'You're outrageous, Laura,' she said.

Laura skewered the largest of the three field mushrooms on Alfred's plate and began to nibble around the edges.

'God, this is good.'

'I thought you weren't hungry?' said Hetty.

'So did I. But apparently I was wrong. I hope you're going to share your steak with me Alfred.'

'Go ahead. Help yourself,' said the American sadly. 'I hope it's not too rare.'

When the salad niçoise with undercooked eggs arrived, Laura was full. The wooden bowl was put in the middle of the table and everyone helped themselves. They ordered two more bottles of wine.

Then Laura said, 'Let's have some coke.'

'Absolutely,' said Henderson. 'Why don't we?'

Alfred had fallen asleep against the picture. He was snoozing with his mouth slightly open. Laura elbowed him in the arm.

'Hey,' she said.

He opened his eyes with a startled expression and automatically pulled down the napkin which was still tucked into his collar.

Laura pointed at her nose.

'Sure,' said Alfred.

He took a small oblong paper package out of his pocket and handed it to her.

'There's a razor blade inside. Be careful you don't cut yourself.'

Laura cleared a space in front of her and opened out the envelope.

Alfred said, 'Aren't you going to the rest room?'

'No one will notice,' said Laura blithely. 'This place is practically empty.'

She held a knife with white powder on the end under Henderson's nose.

'Snort,' she said with an American accent.

One by one everyone round the table followed suit. When Fergus took the cocaine it instantly gave him a sour taste at the back of his throat. He rubbed under his nose nervously in case there were any tell-tale signs of white powder above the lip and looked around. The party presided over by the man with the moustache were talking more quietly. He sensed they had seen. The drug began to give him a mild feeling of euphoria and his anxiety slipped away.

They finished the bottles of wine and ordered brandies and liqueurs. More cocaine was taken. The party at the next table grew still quieter. Alfred began to look depressed. Towards eleven the waitress sat down in the corner and began to fill the salt and pepper canisters. Want to court disaster? a voice taunted him. Why not snort in a restaurant? Oh bugger off, replied another voice. What could happen? At the end of the evening they'd pay the bill. It'd be a bit frosty with sourface in the corner and they'd leave.

Laura began one of her party turns: 'Hetty in love.' This was a parody of the love-sick Hetty — she was as resolutely submissive in love as she was churlish in life — waiting for a boyfriend by the telephone.

'My sweet God and my even sweeter Jesus, will he ever ring?' said Laura dramatically, imitating Hetty's peculiar nasal intonation.

She flung out her arms and accidentally knocked over the glass of crème de menthe frappé which Hetty had been drinking. All of the green liquid emptied onto Hetty's lap.

'You stupid girl,' said Hetty. 'You've wet my lap.'

She rubbed at the stain with a paper napkin but it was thin and didn't absorb.

Hetty said, 'Give me your dress and you can have these.' She pulled at the waistband of her trousers.

Oh-oh, thought Fergus. The sense of alarm was closer, pulsating not faintly this time but powerfully.

Laura stood up and lifted the cream dress she was wearing over her head. She was naked underneath except for a salmon-coloured pair of knickers. His stomach began to curdle.

'I'm not ashamed of my body,' said Laura. What a stupid thing to say, Fergus heard himself thinking. Of course you're not. Otherwise you wouldn't be running around like that.

What about the other guests? he wondered. The sour-faced blonde waitress? Oh if only they hadn't been so rude to her. She was filling a salt cellar like there was no tomorrow. Good. Keep it up. The party next door looked more silent but at least they were talking. Down the end? The couple holding hands hadn't noticed. Thank Christ for passion. The foursome looked amused. Well, they would, wouldn't they?

'I don't think your tits are too small,' said Henderson.

The party at the next table stopped talking altogether.

Laura said, 'Come on then Hetty. I thought you wanted to swap?'

Without getting up from her chair, Hetty began to pull down her floral patterned trousers.

'Coy are we? Don't like to show our legs?' taunted Laura.

The trousers came off in a crumpled heap. Hetty threw them across the table and onto the floor.

Hetty said, 'You've soaked my knickers too, you stupid girl.'

'You want mine?' said Laura.

Hetty shrugged her shoulders ambiguously.

This was it, Fergus thought.

Laura pulled down her knickers and threw them onto Hetty's lap. Laura had rather short legs, a long back and black bushy pubic hair.

'Go on, get 'em off!' she said in a leering tone to her friend.

Fergus' eyes were darting around although he himself was still. The blonde waitress was gone from the corner, leaving a large Cerebos salt after her. The envelope of cocaine was still in the middle of the table. He would have liked to put it in his pocket for safe keeping. But because it wasn't his, he felt inhibited. He glanced at Alfred and saw that the American had closed his eyes and was leaning against the picture. How dare he. He'd brought Laura, so it was bloody well up to him to keep her under control.

She lifted her arms and turned several circles on the floor.

'I feel so free, so free,' she sang. 'Come on Jennifer, swap with me.'

She picked up a tall glass of Perrier water and poured it over Jennifer's head. Fergus watched the water cascading over the freckled face, down the brown hair and onto the pale blue dress, as if in slow motion, followed by the slice of lemon and the half-melted cubes of ice. He heard Laura saying something about everyone changing clothes and saw that she had sat on Henderson's lap and was trying to undo his tie. Could he sign a cheque, leave it on the table and slip away? He put his hand in his pocket and felt that his pen indeed was there. In his mind's eye he could see the cheque in front of him, dated and signed but with the amount left blank. But it wasn't going to work, was it? Slip out now and hope no one noticed. He was up to his neck in it and was just going to have to sit it out.

There was a crackling sound. He knew what that was, a walkie-talkie. He turned in his seat and saw the blue-coated figure of a policeman climbing the stairs, with the sour-faced waitress close behind. Do it, he told himself, and do it fast. He turned back to the table, pushed a wedge of camembert cheese onto the envelope of cocaine and swallowed the lot.

19

In the street outside the Sacred Heart it was chilly. There was a smell of refuse and rotting fish. A couple of women walking along arm in arm stared at them. Fergus followed Alfred and Henderson into the back of one of the police Rovers. The door shut behind with a heavy thump. He had never been in a police car before. It smelt of boiled sweets.

A policeman climbed in.

'What happened?' asked the driver.

'Everyone was just a bit over-emotional,' said the second policeman.

They started to drive. Fergus looked out of the window. Everything seemed to slide by as in a dream. What would they ask him, and did they know what he had swallowed? He remembered the man with the moustache talking to the police and trembled. He looked at the driver in front of him. His dark hair was ragged and unevenly cut.

The police car turned into a yard at the back of the station and they climbed out. There were vehicles parked in a row and a couple of men in white shirts were kicking a football to one another under bright lights. They were brought through a door and down a passage. A sergeant in uniform took their names and addresses and they were separated. Fergus and Alfred were brought upstairs and put on a bench in a corridor. They were told that under no circumstances were they to talk to one another. A very young policeman was left to watch them.

Fergus sat quite still. Now steady yourself, he thought. He tried to concentrate on the noises which he could hear. He identified the sound of motor cars below in the yard, the gurgling of pipes in a nearby cistern, the ring of the telephone and the click-click of shoes on linoleum.

Alfred asked to go to the lavatory. He was pointed towards a door marked 'Men'. After Alfred had gone in, a man in a suit appeared carrying a file.

'Mr,' he looked at the file, 'Fergus Maguire,' he said, reading the name written on the front.

'Yes,' said Fergus. This was it. They'd courted disaster, and now here was the consequence. He was going to be charged with a serious crime.

The man introduced himself as Curry.

Fergus followed him down the corridor and into a room. It was bare with a grille over the window and a table and two chairs bolted to the middle of the floor.

'Sit down.'

Fergus took the seat with its back to the window and Curry sat opposite him.

Fergus said, 'Are you *Mr* Curry?' Get them talking. That was best.

'Mr Curry will be fine. Or detective-sergeant.'

Curry opened the file. Inside there was a piece of paper a quarter covered with typed script and signed underneath. What could that be? Fergus tried to read the upside-down signature and then found that Curry had caught him at it. He blushed. Curry shut the file.

'We all do stupid things from time to time,' said Curry. 'We all drink too much sometimes and get carried away. Even I've done that in my time. Then there are the really stupid things, the criminal things. They're in another league altogether. You and your party were taking drugs this evening, weren't you?'

Curry was looking across the table at him without blinking.

'I think I'm entitled to call a solicitor,' said Fergus. Then he added, 'Aren't I?' That was polite, he thought, which was good. He had to avoid being cocky. On the other hand, he also had to steer clear of being sycophantic.

'Mr Maguire, if we want to, we can put you on the toilet for a week and wait for what will to come out.'

Fergus felt his mouth going dry.

'We've had a full statement. Do you smoke?'

With a shaking hand Fergus took a cigarette from the packet which Curry was holding out to him. A second later the detective lit the end.

'I'm going to give you a few minutes to think,' said Curry standing up, 'and when I come back I want you to tell me exactly what happened.'

Curry went out and the young-looking policeman came in. He took up position by the light switch. Fergus smoked. The tobacco was hot and strong. Curry had left the file on the table-top, closed naturally. He tried to decide what he was going to do but couldn't get his mind to focus. All that he could do was to look at his name on the file which was staring up at him.

The door opened and Curry came back in again. Co-operate and answer whatever questions the man asks, Fergus said to himself. The young policeman went outside.

Curry stubbed his cigarette on the floor and sat down.

Fergus said, 'I'm terribly sorry about what happened.'

'You don't know how happy I am to hear you say that. Are you Irish?'

Fergus nodded.

'I thought I recognised the brogue. Do you mind if I call you Fergus?'

'No.' He didn't mind what Curry called him.

'I'm happy to tell you, Fergus, my superior has decided not to press charges.'

This couldn't be true. Fallen down a hole? Here's a rope. You didn't get into this sort of trouble only to be got out of it so easily.

67

'Does that mean I can go?'

'I want to give you some advice, Fergus.'

For the first time since the interview had started, Fergus had a good look at the man. Curry had brown hair and brown eyes and sallow skin. He also had a small mark in the middle of his nose like a cut. The whole effect was strangely inhuman and intimidating.

'Never do what you did tonight, again.' The detective spoke slowly, emphasising each of the words as if he was speaking to someone who was deaf. 'Next time you won't find us so bloody lenient.'

Curry stared at him and Fergus nodded emphatically. Just agree to anything, he told himself, and get out of there.

'Do you know Miss Shellgate and the others well?'

'Laura, Miss Shellgate, I know very well. She's an old girlfriend. Henderson is my oldest friend; we were at school together. The other two girls I hardly know and I'd never met the American before this evening,' said Fergus in a rush.

'I don't think you're going round with a very nice crowd of people, Fergus,' said the detective. 'I want you to stop seeing all of them. A nice young man like you — they're right out of your class. You should stick to your own.'

'You're right,' said Fergus, 'I'll do as you say. It's very good advice.'

'I know,' said Curry. 'We speak the same language,' he continued. 'We understand each other.'

He wrote a telephone number on a piece of paper and handed it across.

'If you have any information, call us. You don't need to mention your name. It's confidential. You owe us one. You could lead us to the big boys. You know what I mean?'

Fergus nodded. He was beginning to feel nauseous.

20

The others were waiting downstairs. A policewoman escorted them to the front and they left by the main entrance. As soon as his foot touched the pavement, Fergus felt his mind clearing — it was a sense of melting and unfreezing — and his thoughts began to race. Why had they been released just like that? Why hadn't they been charged? The business of putting him on the lavatory had obviously been a crude threat. A blood test would have settled it. They'd started applying pressure and then taken it off. Finally, they'd asked him to collaborate.

'What happened?' asked Henderson quietly. 'We thought they were giving you the fifth degree.'

Fergus said, 'It wasn't very pleasant. They want me to help them. They gave me this number to ring if I have any information.'

They began to walk. The street lamps were white and stretched away like a necklace of light. Everyone else, judging by their accounts, had been reprimanded. Everyone felt subdued.

'What time is it?' asked Hetty.

Laura said, 'I know I won't be able to sleep tonight.'

'It's half past one,' said Alfred.

'There's the Dixons' party,' said Laura. 'Shall we go?'

Fergus said, 'They were going to put me on the lavatory and wait for it to come out.'

'My detective was dishy,' said Laura, 'what was yours like, Jennifer?'

'I don't want to talk about it,' replied Jennifer. 'Mine was a woman and she was a creep.'

They hailed a taxi and drove down to Kensington High Street. Fergus, wedged in the corner, felt Jennifer pressing against him.

'Look over there, look at that,' said Henderson.

Everyone turned. On the pavement a young woman was leading a man with a blindfold over his eyes.

'Do you suppose they're drunk?' asked Alfred.

With his arm on the woman's shoulder and his head held high, the man reminded Fergus of the First World War, the long lines of men blindly following one another along muddy roads, each with a hand on the shoulder of the man in front.

'Yes,' said Laura. 'How does it go?'

> 'Three blind mice,
> See how they run?
> The cook with the carving knife . . . .'

'No, no,' said Henderson.

> 'They all ran after the farmer's wife,
> Who cut off their tails with a carving knife,
> Did you ever see such a thing in your life?
> As three blind mice?'

By the Albert Hall they turned down Gloucester Road. Fergus could feel something in his stomach. It was a stretching sensation in his muscles on either side of his belly button. He pulled down the window and cold air rushed in. After a moment or two he began to feel better.

'Are you feeling all right?' asked Jennifer.

'I feel okay. I just felt a bit odd that's all,' he said.

'You were a hero,' said Laura.

Everyone murmured agreement.

'You've got us out of a potentially very nasty situation,' said Alfred. 'Especially me.'

'Three cheers for Fergus . . . .' said Laura.

Their voices chorused and Jennifer took him by the hand and squeezed. Fergus found himself enjoying her touch.

The taxi pulled up in front of a row of stucco houses. They all clambered out. While the fare was being settled, Fergus wandered over to the railings that ran round the communal garden. A big November moon hung in the sky, pearly white with pale grey shadings. The panic which had overwhelmed him in the police station had almost vanished and he didn't feel physically peculiar any longer. What he felt now was a distinct sense, half made up of anxiety, half made up of gratitude, that he'd courted disaster and been just oh so lucky to have got away with it. He felt as he imagined one felt after running for an aeroplane and catching it at the very last moment, only worse. Then he thought about Curry with his brown face and cut nose. He still had the paper in his pocket. He drew it out and stared at the red biro numbers. Even though he couldn't help the police, the very idea of any sort of association made him tremble. It reminded him of the women with shorn heads after the liberation of France, terrified amidst jeering crowds, shielding babies fathered by the just-departed Germans. He tore up the paper and scattered the confetti-sized pieces on the flower-bed beyond the railings.

A voice called, 'Come on, Fergus.'

70

He followed his party through a heavy glass door embellished with wrought iron. They climbed a first flight of stairs and rounded the corner. Further steps swept away to a landing. A girl of about twenty years of age sat at the top. She was wearing a strapless gown with a man's dinner jacket draped over her bare shoulders. Henderson ran forward, lifted her up and kissed her. Jennifer knew her too. When Fergus reached the top she was introduced to him as Hilary. After he had shaken her hand, he looked around. He could hear Hilary answering questions about who was at the party. He saw waiters in white tie and heard laughter in rooms leading off the landing. Most of the guests were in evening dress.

'I don't think I'm really dressed for this,' he said to Henderson quietly.

'Nor am I. But no one will notice. They'll just put it down to our youth.'

A gangling middle-aged man in a dinner shirt but no jacket crept up and pushed against Hilary's knees from behind, causing her momentarily to look as though she were about to fall.

'Oh, it's you Clive,' she said, at once weary and tart.

'Hello Clive,' said Jennifer.

'Greetings,' said Henderson coolly, giving Clive a sidelong look.

'This is my fiancé,' said Hilary and Fergus shook Clive by the hand.

'Where's the ring darlin',' shouted Laura. She lifted up Hilary's hand. On the ring finger there was a thin gold band with a diamond at the top.

'Oh, very flashy.' She spoke in an appalling mock-cockney accent. 'Must have cost our Clive a few bob. Or did he buy it on hire purchase? Anyway, you must be very happy dear. I always say, a girl's quite naked, starkers, until she's got that ring on . . . .'

Fergus wandered into a room with a strong smell of cigar smoke.

'With ice,' he said, to the barman behind the trestle table, pointing at the bottle of Famous Grouse. Cubes clinking in his glass, he drifted through an arch to a long room from which the balcony led off. On an empty table there were some cigarettes in a glass. They reminded him of conductors' batons. He took one and lit it.

'Hello. I'm the hostess. Who are you?'

71

Fergus turned round and saw a large fat woman with an orchid in her hair.

'I'm Fergus,' he said. Then he added, 'Maguire.'

'How do you do. Are you enjoying yourself? Have you had a drink?'

He held up the tumbler. 'Yes, thank you.'

'Are you an old friend of my daughter's?'

'No, new,' he lied.

'Where did you meet her? Through work?'

'No. At a party.'

'It's so strange for me as her mother. All these friends and I don't know any of them. I suppose that's what they call the generation gap. I hope you enjoy yourself.'

Fergus nodded goodbye and she walked away, touching her orchid to make certain it was in place. Mrs Dixon was short and wide, wearing a tulip shaped dress which stopped above her knee, and a black velvet headband to secure her flower.

Fergus went through the french windows and into the conservatory which ran along the balcony. A few guests sat on cushions among the potted plants. Glowing chinese lanterns hung from the ceiling. He could smell wax and hear the candles guttering. He went over to the balustrade and looked through the glass across to the communal garden. The leaves of the trees, the bushes and the grass were dark, almost black, but the sandy path which ran inside the railings was glimmering palely in the moonlight. A man was walking his dog.

After he had finished his cigarette Fergus threw it out of the window and it was then he noticed Hilary at the other end of the balcony, no longer with the dinner jacket on her shoulders. She was neither short nor tall, with pale blonde bobbed hair. Her dress was black and it made her bare, bony shoulders and her long neck seem peculiarly white. She was stroking one of her long earrings and staring into the street. The impression was quite different from the initial one.

He finished his drink and started to suck the spindles of ice that were left. He wanted another but he did not want to move away in case he lost the opportunity of starting a conversation. Hilary was fumbling with her small clutch handbag. She found a cigarette, lit it and sat down on the edge of the balustrade to smoke. She performed these actions slowly, as if she was tired.

Fergus rushed back to the trestle, got another whisky, took two more cigarettes from the glass and strolled back onto the balcony.

'I'm sorry to trouble you,' he said, holding a cigarette up. 'Do you have a light?'

'You'll have to forgive the lighter,' she said, as she took it out of her bag. There was a photograph of a naked Tahitian girl on the side with blue sea stretching behind her.

Fergus said, 'I think it's great.'

'It's usually the men who object nowadays. My girlfriends think it's quite sweet.'

The end of his cigarette glowed. 'You met me a few minutes ago,' he said. 'I'm called Fergus.'

'I'm called Hilary Lumley, I think.'

'You think?'

'I can't even remember what I was doing ten minutes ago, so don't expect me to remember my name.'

'Okay,' Fergus said, 'where were you ten minutes ago?'

'Sitting on the landing, meeting you.'

He shrugged his shoulders. 'I can detect a lie at a hundred paces. One of the benefits of a Catholic education.' He was being pretentious, he thought. If anyone had tried that on him at a party he'd have made his excuses and walked away.

She looked up at him. She had a wide face and high cheekbones. Her eyes were very blue and she had a large, hooked nose which was strangely beautiful. Her mouth was very red because of the lipstick which she was wearing and there was some on the end of her cigarette. On one of her temples he could see a blue vein. It was his impression that her skin, pale and white, was thinner than most skins.

'You haven't told me your surname,' she said. 'I don't like this first-names-only business. I like a surname. I can remember a surname.'

'Maguire.'

'Oh. Maguire.'

He felt someone touching his arm.

'There you are,' said a voice.

He turned around. It was Jennifer. On the side of her head she was wearing a small, pointed carnival hat. He was faintly annoyed by her appearance and the fact that she had found him.

73

Jennifer said, 'Hello, Hilary. I've been looking for him everywhere, and I suppose he's been out here on the balcony all the time?'

Hilary said, 'Had a nice day, Jennifer?'

'So, so.'

Hilary opened a window and her cigarette arched like a falling star into the street. 'That's good.'

Jennifer said, 'Have you heard from our man in Paris today?'

'I thought he was in Madrid.'

'I heard he was in Paris. Can I steal him away?'

'Who?'

'Fergus.'

Hilary looked at Fergus again. 'I don't own you. Do I?'

He wanted to touch her skin. He imagined it would be slightly cooler than anyone else's and ever so slightly downy, or furry, like the skin of a peach.

Fergus said, 'No. I'm a free man.'

Hilary said, 'I wish I was a free woman.'

Fergus followed Jennifer through the french windows.

'Did you want to talk to her?' Jennifer asked.

'She's nice.'

'I'm sorry. I thought you looked as though you needed rescuing.'

Nonsense, he thought. None the less, there was something about her coming to find him that gave him a warm glow of pleasure.

She took him by the arm and they began to walk towards the arch. A young man in a shirt with a ribbed front was flicking peanuts up into the air and catching them in his mouth.

'Do you want another drink?' asked Fergus pointing towards the trestle.

Jennifer said, 'That would be nice. Then we could go home.'

The barman poured them two whiskies. As he handed over the glasses he nodded towards the circle of older people around the fireplace including Mrs Dixon.

'They've been re-fighting all the wars of the last forty years. I suppose it keeps 'em happy, God bless 'em.'

They ambled to the middle of the room and stood awkwardly drinking. Jennifer knew Mrs Dixon and wanted to go and say something. But the opportunity to break into the ring of talkers never offered itself.

Finally Fergus said, 'Let's go.'

They put their glasses on the yellow stone floor of the landing and began to go down the stairs.

'Jennifer. You're going without saying hello,' sounded a voice behind them.

It was the hostess. They went back up the stairs.

'I didn't want to interrupt just now,' said Jennifer. 'Thank you. It was a lovely, lovely party.'

'How's your mother?' The orchid had slipped down from the side of Mrs Dixon's head to behind her left ear. It looked like an earmuff worn askew.

'She's very well thank you,' said Jennifer.

'Give her my regards if you ever see her. Do come again.' Her face creased. 'Goodbye Maurice.'

Fergus and Jennifer went down the stairs sedately until they rounded the corner. Then they began to accelerate.

In the hall the woman who had let them in opened the door for them.

'So pleased you could come,' she said.

They stepped out into the night air and the door shut behind them.

'Goodbye Maurice,' said Jennifer imitating the hostess's reedy voice and touching her hair where the orchid was.

'Yes, goodbye Jennifer and Maurice,' said a voice above them.

Fergus looked up and saw the squat, wide figure of Mrs Dixon with the slipped orchid looking down from the conservatory through an open window. She was waving a small white handkerchief like a character in a silent film. She had surely heard Jennifer's imitation, he thought. Jennifer started to laugh.

He took her by the elbow and they began to run. As they ran Jennifer laughed louder. When they reached the corner they stopped and turned round. The hostess was gone but Fergus thought he could make out the tall outline of Hilary staring down the street after them.

He took Jennifer by the arm and they hurried out of sight.

75

21

They went into a hotel in Knightsbridge to buy cigarettes. The night porter, who was busy splashing around in the fountain, directed them to the machine by the staff entrance. After they had trickled the change through the slot, the tray refused to come out. Jennifer hit the glass front several times. A man appeared and remonstrated with her about her treatment of private property. At that moment Fergus, who had continued tugging, managed to release the tray and Jennifer mumbled angrily at the man, 'You stupid berk.' When challenged by the man who, it turned out, was the hotel detective, to repeat what she had said, she replied without a pause, 'If you must know, what I said was, "Well done Dirk." My boyfriend's name is Dirk, you see, and because he got the machine to work I said "Well done Dirk".' She pointed at Fergus to emphasise her point.

They fled back to the foyer and the porter, now sitting in his wellington boots on the edge of the fountain, showed them a huge dead goldfish which he had in a plastic bag.

'A load of yahoos pissed in here after a party last week. All the fish died,' he explained.

He put down the carcass and wiped his fingers on his apron. The fish scales left a trace like the smear of a snail.

'You know, this is a sad land,' he said, 'where only the ghosts are good.'

They went back outside and Fergus asked Jennifer if she always answered back as she had to the hotel detective.

'I hate people like him. They make my blood boil,' she said.

'I bet you never got on with your teachers.'

'Nope.'

'Always get into an argument at Customs?'

'Absolutely.'

'Hate the sight of a uniform?'

'Unquestionably.'

At least she was funny about it, he thought.

They hailed a taxi and Jennifer gave the driver her address. They climbed in and it rattled off. On the bottoms of the jumpseats there were advertisements for duty-free shopping at Heathrow. Fergus found Jennifer's hand. She returned his squeezes. Would they sleep together? he wondered. He pictured her head on the pillow. The earlier part of the evening and Curry were almost forgotten.

The taxi pulled up in front of a mansion block in Battersea. The driver paid, they went up to her flat. Jennifer brought him to the living room and said she had to rush to the lavatory. He sat on the sofa and started to thumb through an old copy of *Vogue*. He found an article on underground stations which he began to read. He heard the sound of a key in the hall door and a moment later a blonde head peeped into the room. No one could have been more surprised than he, when he saw that it was Hilary.

'Oh, hello,' she said. 'You left the party before us. Have you got a cigarette?'

'I didn't know you shared a flat with Jennifer.'

'Oh. Didn't you?'

While Fergus felt in his pockets, she took a package down from the mantelpiece and opened it.

'Do you like these?' She showed him a pile of square felt table mats stitched in red around the edges and each with a brown bear in the middle.

'They come from the Russian shop. They're an early engagement present from my mother.'

'Lovely.'

'I collect Russian dolls. I have eighty-three at home.'

Fergus handed her a cigarette and lit it. 'So you're getting married? When did all this happen?'

'The engagement party was last week.'

'Who's the lucky man?'

'He's called Clive. You met him earlier. At the party. I thought I was the person who forgot things and you were the one who remembered them.'

'Of course I did. When's it to be?'

'Two months' time, three months' time, and don't say that's too soon.'

'Did I say anything?'

'No.'

'There you go,' he said.

'We decided long drawn-out engagements aren't worth it. Don't you agree?'

'I've never been engaged.'

'Why wait a year if you've made your mind up? Why not just go for it as Clive says. We'll only live together as if we were married anyway. Don't you agree?'

'If you say so, you must be right.'

'What time is it?'

'It's after two o'clock.'

'Unfortunately, my parents don't see it that way. We're going down to see them this weekend. Clive's going to try to talk some sense into them.'

The lavatory flushed and they fell silent. Jennifer reappeared.

'Want a drink?' she asked. She flopped down on the sofa beside him. 'My God that light is bright.'

They all squinted at the white globe lampshade hanging from the middle of the ceiling.

'Where's Clive?'

'Parking,' replied Hilary.

'It's a nightmare around here,' explained Jennifer. Then she said, 'I can offer you a gin martini.'

He nodded.

'All right then. The girls will make the drinks. Come on Hilary.'

They went out and left him alone. Hilary's unexpected appearance threatened to spoil everything. Why had Jennifer taken her off to the kitchen? he asked himself. Was she at that moment instructing her flatmate to stick with them? To prevent anything from happening? Or perhaps Hilary was being given the order to drink up in five minutes and clear off, turning off the light as she went? Hardly likely.

The entryphone buzzed in the hall and a few minutes later the door into the living room opened again and in came Clive. Over his dinner jacket he was wearing an absurd striped woollen scarf which hung down to his knees.

'Christ I feel ghastly,' he said, sinking into the armchair. 'I mixed my drinks this evening in a quite disgusting manner. Sherry, wine, Cointreau and champagne. And tomorrow I've got a three-hour drive and then the whole bloody day with Hilary's parents who think I'm a cradle snatcher. Just think of that on a hangover. And for Christ's sake, it's not as if I'm that old. I'm only forty.'

He leant back in the armchair, put his hands behind his head and a moment later began to snore softly.

Fergus went back to his article and began to read a description of the beauties of Baker Street underground station. After a few minutes, there was laughter outside and Jennifer and Hilary appeared with a tray. They had mixed the drink in a milk bottle and now poured it into the glasses through a tea strainer.

'Where's my olive?' Fergus asked Jennifer when she handed him his.

'My fiancé snores,' said Hilary, settling on the arm of his chair beside his sleeping form.

Hilary and Jennifer began to talk about Hilary's imminent visit to her parents and the coming wedding. Fergus asked what hymns Hilary was going to have at her service.

'I don't know any hymns,' she replied.

He decided not to ask any more questions and thought about Jennifer instead. Should he linger or call for a taxi and say airily on the way out he would telephone her soon? The effect of the cocaine had stayed in his stomach, adding to his irritation.

Just as he decided he would leave, Hilary sprang to her feet, roused Clive and took him away. Jennifer came and sat by him on the sofa. She told him how pleased she was they had met. When they drained the glasses of their second martinis, Jennifer closed her eyes and held her face towards him. Her make-up had worn thin and she looked tired.

Fergus bent forward, closing his eyes. His lips found hers. Her tongue was small and pointed. It tasted of gin. As he kissed Jennifer moved her head from side to side and made small noises of passion. He undid the buttons at the front of her dress and felt her breasts. Through the gossamer material of her brassière her nipples grew hard.

'What time is it?' asked Jennifer.

They separated from their embrace and Fergus looked at his watch.

'It's round about three,' he said.

'How am I going to get up tomorrow?' she asked.

'I'll wake you.'

'I have the curse. It's just bloody started.'

That explained the bathroom.

'Well,' he said, 'we can hold each other.'

She drained her glass and gave him a sidelong glance.

'You don't think Laura will mind?'

'No, why should she?'

'Yes, why should she? You don't go out any more.'

She showed him the bedroom and he went to brush his teeth. When he came out he heard her in the kitchen washing glasses.

He went through to her bedroom and found himself in a square room with a large four-poster bed standing against the far wall. There was a dressing table covered with make-up and a boxed edition of Beatrix Potter on the window ledge. He undressed and climbed into the bed. The sheets were starched and the stuffed rabbit on the pillow smelt of shampoo. He began to drift towards sleep.

The door clicked shut and Jennifer appeared beside him.

'I see you've met Thumper,' she said pointing to the rabbit.

She was naked. He glanced at her groin and saw the tell-tale string of a tampax hanging down, white amidst the black hair. He felt vaguely disappointed.

'Yes. Thumper and I have been having a long conversation about you. Past boyfriends.'

'Oh Thumper, I hope you were discreet.'

She turned off the light and climbed in beside him. They kissed one another. She had a soft, warm body. Fergus felt an erection growing and so did she. She made pretend eating noises and slid under the covers. He opened his legs and felt her warm mouth around his sex and her hands cupping his testicles. She moved her head up and down. He opened his eyes and saw her shape beneath the covers. He reached below and took hold of her by the back of the head, entwining his fingers in her hair. He closed his eyes. Some moments later his semen came out. He froze and so did she. He lay still. So did she. He could feel himself shrinking. She opened her mouth and he fell out of her sideways. He felt her kissing him tenderly. She came out from under the covers making the imitation eating noises she'd made before.

'You taste, you taste woody,' she said.

They kissed and curled up beside each other.

'Bloody Laura, she's a walking disaster,' muttered Jennifer.

Side by side in the darkness they laughed quietly.

'Was she always like that?'

'Absolutely.'

'Was that why you and her stopped?'

'That and the Irish Sea.'

Jennifer rolled away and nestled with her stomach against his back.

'Mhhh . . . . Goodnight.'

He closed his eyes. Their intimacy puzzled him. But before he could pursue the thought, he was asleep.

22

At one o'clock Martin-Smith left the office for lunch. Fergus looked up Arthur Books in his address book and dialled the number. A young woman answered the telephone. Fergus asked for Jennifer.

'She's not here.'

'Do you know where she is?'

'It's after one. Where else do you think she is? She's at lunch of course. This is England. Remember?'

'When do you expect her back?'

'No idea.'

'Are you the receptionist?'

'No. I just answer the telephone.'

'May I leave a message?'

'I don't have a pencil. It'll have to be a simple one.'

'Would you ask Jennifer to call Fergus Maguire? She knows the number.'

The girl at the other end put down the telephone.

'Idiot,' muttered Fergus.

He picked up *The Torture Papers* and sat back in his chair. The book was printed on porous paper which was shedding like whitewash. He opened it thirty pages from the start and read:

. . . sweating palms, abdominal pains, irregular bowel movements, sleeplessness, tiredness and certain problems in the sex
area had all begun to trouble me. But where had they come
from? I was a healthy man. I had healthy instincts. These things
didn't happen to chartered accountants. I consulted my doctor.
He gave me a check up and asked the standard questions. In all
respects I was normal. 'Has anything unusual happened to you
recently Mr Wiggins?' he then asked.

'Unusual?' I mused. 'No. I don't think so.'

'You haven't knocked your head, had a slight bump in your
car or anything like that?'

'No,' I said.

At that moment my doctor answered the telephone.

As he talked into the receiver I looked around. On his desk
there was a calendar from a pharmaceutical company. His
blotter was covered with spidery shapes where he had blotted his
prescriptions. I looked at the examination couch covered with a
coarse covering of paper which came off a roll, and then out of
the window. All I could see were the backs of town houses,
drainpipes, windows, doorways and small gardens. It was
autumn and someone somewhere was burning leaves. I could see
the smoke.

'Has anything unusual happened to you lately?' My doctor's
words sounded in my ears. 'Has anything unusual happened Mr
Wiggins?'

Yes, it had. I thought back to the police station, the night I
had spent in the cells, waking up in the morning and not knowing
what had happened. But that had been months before. Water
under the bridge.

It was only later that I discovered how wrong was my
conclusion.

Fergus liked the description of the doctor's consulting room but
lost confidence at the police station. Mr Wiggins was a madman,
he decided, though as madmen went, and Fergus had come across
quite a number in his work, Mr Wiggins was probably more
interesting.

He left the office and took the lift to the ground floor. Merci-
fully Jack was nowhere to be seen. Fergus went outside. A line of

office workers queued in the doorway of a sandwich bar, muffled in coats, breath curling from their nostrils. In the window of a Japanese restaurant there were *sushi* dishes reproduced in plastic. They reminded him of liquorice allsorts. He turned down an alley. On one side there was a brick building with a notice: *Total Striptease. Girls undressed to thrill.* A woman in a black brassière leant out of a window above. He was surprised she didn't feel the cold.

'Looking for a girl, sir?' the woman called.

'No, thanks,' said Fergus and turned into the Atlanta Sandwich Bar opposite.

'What's it to be?' asked the owner, cleaning a long knife with a cloth. He was a short, gruff-sounding man with a cataract in one eye.

Fergus ordered a crab salad sandwich on brown bread with onion and black pepper. Whilst the proprietor made it up he turned round, put his elbows on the counter and looked out of the window. There were two people in the doorway of the strip club: a blonde on a stool wearing stockings and a man with a Mediterranean complexion. They were looking over their shoulders towards the door behind which led into the theatre. A figure was slipping through and Fergus was certain he recognised the profile carrying the briefcase. It was Mr Wiggins.

23

In the middle of the afternoon Jennifer rang. They exchanged pleasantries for a few moments and then Jennifer said, 'What are doing just now?'

'Right now?'

'Yes.'

'Reading a book left here by a lunatic.'

'And?'

'It's called *The Torture Papers*.'

'Yes . . . .'

'It's written by a looney called Wiggins who thinks he's being controlled by the police.'

'. . . ?'

'Literally, with electrodes. But it's much better if I read his story than if I tell you.'

'. . . .'

'He's arrested for speeding and taken to a police station in Worcestershire. This is twenty years ago. He's been drinking, so he has to spend the night there.'

'How old is he at this point?'

'Thirties, I'd guess. They take away his shoelaces and bring him to his cell. The door clangs behind him. You have the picture?'

'. . . .'

'This is what he says:

"... Rest was what I needed if I was going to face the Magistrate. Accordingly, I curled up on my pallet and fell into a peaceful and dreamless sleep. . . .

At least I thought it was. Now I know that it was neither.

The tea and the biscuits which I had been given were laced with strong sedatives. Once they had taken their effect, I was wheeled from the cell on a trolley to an operating theatre in the basement of the station. Here, the doctor who had taken my blood sample was waiting. My cranium was removed and four small electrodes inserted into my brain. My cranium was then replaced and my skin sewn up with tiny little stitches. Dissolving thread was used so there would be no tell-tale signs. Then, none the wiser, I was returned to my cell.

'He's making it up,' I can hear one reader saying . . . ."

'No, Mr Wiggins,' interjected Fergus.

"'I can see another shaking his head. . . ."

'No, Mr Wiggins.' Fergus was rather enjoying his reading.

"But if it isn't true, why would I go to the bother of writing this book and printing it myself? I can promise you, this required no small amount of time, effort and expense. . . ."

84

'Now, Jennifer,' said Fergus, 'here comes the really classic section.

> "If I were simply a liar who told preposterous stories, would I have the patience for this? No. It's only because I am describing the truth, that I have been prepared to go to these lengths. The lie has been told for too long. Now it is time for a citizen to stand up and say, 'Enough,' and I am such a citizen."'

'Don't we have any work to do?' asked Martin-Smith from his desk.

'Mind your own business,' replied Fergus. Then he continued to Jennifer, 'It's extraordinary, isn't it? And it goes on in the same vein. I'll read you some more.'

He turned over the pages.

'Wiggins goes to court the next morning. He's found guilty, fined and his licence is taken away. All right?'

'. . . .'

'He leaves the court in a daze and starts wondering about how he's going to break the news to mother, when . . . . Guess what?'

'. . . ?'

'After the operation it could only be God:

> ". . . Inside the church there wasn't a soul. I sat down on a pew. It was all quiet and spiritual. Suddenly I detected a cold wind moving across my back. I was not alone. Involuntarily, I looked up at Jesus on his cross. A great white light burnt in front of my eyes and I heard His voice.
>
> 'Charlie,' he said, 'last night when you were asleep, you were operated upon. The purpose was to turn you into a man who will do the bidding of certain persons. In time you will find out all the details. You will discover too the terrible side-effects of the operation, that it has unmanned you. As soon as you are in the full possession of these facts, you must tell the world. One day you will be a famous man; my trust is with you.'"

'So,' said Fergus, 'guess what his first decision is?'

'I don't know.'

'He decides he's not going to tell his mother he spent the night in a police cell. And he's going to tell a lie, because, and I quote: "I had to tell a small untruth in the cause of the greater absolute truth." Poor Mr Wiggins. One night in the cells and Jesus starts to speak to him from the cross.'

There was a silence.

'Are you still there?' he asked.

'Yes.'

He lowered his voice.

'Really, one shouldn't laugh. When we had our little experience I felt as if everything I knew had vanished and I was completely lost. I was the most frightened I've ever been. A man like Mr Wiggins, I suppose, is the sort who just doesn't recover. When I think about this book and what happened to us, I keep remembering a quotation I read years ago: "A stranger punches a law-abiding citizen in the street and the victim goes nuts" or something like that. It was in a book about American detective novels. We're so frail it only takes the smallest thing to send us haywire. Or some of us anyway.'

'I think you ought to throw that book away. It gives me the creeps.'

After a month of knowing Jennifer he was able to judge her tone. This was not a joke. 'Okay,' he said.

He held the receiver to the wastepaper bin. The book dropped in with a clang.

'No sooner said than done. Would you like a drink later?'

They made the arrangements and rang off.

After putting down the receiver, Fergus thought with pleasure of the evening ahead.

24

Fergus looked at Jennifer who in turn was staring at the seven Scrabble letters in front of her. She lifted her eyes from the plastic holder on which they rested to the board, moving her lips silently. Her brow furrowed.

'Bugger.'

'You've had at least five minutes.'

'If there was a free "s" I could make "weddings".'

Fergus stared at the board, at the upside-down words running up and down and across. He could hear the clock in the corner, ticking away on Atlas' shoulders, while the gas heater hissed at the door. Outside the streets were quiet; the lull before the pubs closed.

'Six minutes.'

She flapped her hands and said, 'Don't rush me.'

She struck a match. The phosphorus flared. The flame went to the end of her cigarette. A hard flick of the thumb and it was out. Tossed into the metal ashtray, it clinked against the sides.

'I've got a problem.'

Fergus was mixing his own letters around on the table top, hoping that out of the confusion a word would leap up at him.

'Yes.'

'Hilary's left lists of what she wants for her wedding. I rung up the shops this morning. All the cheap things have gone and I can't possibly afford what's left and there's blinking Christmas as well coming up. Anyway, what's a good cheap wedding present?'

'Dunno. A tea cosy?'

'Ha-ha. I think I'm going to have to make "wed". Pathetic isn't it?'

He went over to the window and put his brow against the cold glass. A Vauxhall Cavalier was on the far side of the road.

'Jennifer?'

'What is it?'

Her chair scraped back. A moment later she was beside him.

'I keep seeing that car over there with the men inside. It makes me feel nervous.'

At that moment a woman came out of the laundrette, leant on the car roof and began to speak to the driver.

'What's odd? They've obviously come for her or something. Don't think about it.' There was reassurance in her words.

Jennifer went back to her chair and sat down.

'I can make "dew" of course, that way I'll get more for my "w".'

He was still looking through the window. The woman was

laughing with her head thrown back. Her hair was tossing and her body shook. It looked so innocent and perfectly normal. What had he been worrying about? he asked himself. His were just random sightings which he had connected up as if they had some greater significance. Once again his anxious nature was colouring ordinary and quite explicable events.

He clicked his teeth together.

'It's probably just my imagination,' he said.

'Eleven,' replied Jennifer, 'pathetic, but I'm going to catch up.'

As she marked up her score he sat down.

'You're winning but only by twenty and we've a long way to go.'

He smiled and began to move his tiles up and down like abacus counters.

25

'That is the day of our wedding,' said Mrs Singh.

The colour photograph on the flickering television showed a courtyard. Everyone in the picture was sitting on the ground. In the middle were the bride and bridegroom. Mrs Singh wore a sari; her husband a light-coloured Nehru suit.

'Very good day but much money,' Mr Singh said from the sofa behind.

'And this?' asked Fergus, pointing.

The second photograph showed a young boy with a garland of flowers around his cropped head.

'That is Ravi,' Mrs Singh said, 'my eldest.'

Ravi, towards whom she gestured, was lying in the corner with his brother. From the Pacman game just visible between the shoulders of the boys came strange electronic noises.

'This is after his *dvija*,' Mrs Singh continued, picking up the photograph. 'This was when, in our religion, he became twice born.'

'Very good day when we married but much money,' Mr Singh repeated.

They turned to face him. He was sitting on a patterned sofa with his legs stretching out in front of him.

'Much money.'

'You were married here? In England?' Fergus asked politely.

'Home,' replied Mr Singh. He pointed over his shoulder.

Mrs Singh glided from the room. Fergus accepted the offer of a Special Brew from her husband. The drink came in a heavy tumbler which he imagined was a free gift from a garage.

'Sit,' said Mr Singh.

Fergus settled himself in an armchair. The rust-coloured design showed greenery and ferns. The sound of clattering plates came through the wall from the kitchen. Mr Singh told a long story about a break-in. All Mrs Singh's jewellery had been stolen. The next day Mr Singh had gone out and bought replacements for everything. This proved what a good husband he was.

'Look,' said Mr Singh, suddenly pointing at the television.

Fergus looked across. On the screen was a man's face. The camera was moving slowly towards him and a voice could be heard on the sound track.

'Shhh,' said Mr Singh, pointing at the set. 'He's thinking.' He brought a finger to his lips.

Mr Singh started to discuss England. Life was hard. Money was hard. But it was a good country. Better than where he was from. Fergus demurred. What about the beauty of India? Its ancient history? Its long-established culture?

No, countered Mr Singh, that was for the birds.

He liked to go there. Yes. He missed his family, especially his parents. Yes. But home was Britain. Then Mr Singh started to describe his first job. This was in an electronics factory near Hounslow. Born and raised in a little village, he'd never worked with machines before coming to Britain and his workmates had made him believe for a while there were people inside them.

Fergus listened and stared at the shelves in the corner. Among the knick-knacks he noticed a flamingo dancer with a flame-red skirt, a plastic motorcycle assembled from a kit and a photograph of a Hindu deity who was half-male, half-female.

The door opened and in came Mrs Singh. She was followed by a young girl who Fergus thought looked about sixteen years old.

They set the trays they were carrying on low brass tables. Fergus stood up. The girl was introduced to him as a cousin. Her name was Mira. She shook his hand standing as far back from him as she could. She had a small face and a prominent nose and there was a fine down of black hair at the edge of her cheeks. She wore a skirt with a wide belt and a blouse with a wide collar. From the food on the trays drifted the smell of cumin and ginger.

They all sat down. To eat there were little pastries with spicy fillings and small pieces of red chicken. The drink in the jug was a thin sour yoghurt. Fergus accepted another Special Brew and when Mira returned with it from the kitchen, Mr Singh insisted on clinking glasses with him and saying 'Cheers'.

Towards ten Fergus said he would have to go. From the bottom shelf Mrs Singh took two small shapes wrapped in Christmas paper. Though they were Hindu, she explained, that didn't stop them joining in with Christmas. Fergus was relieved he hadn't come without a present. At that moment it was on the sideboard. It was a history of Ireland which the booksellers had wrapped in brown paper. He had handed it over the moment he'd arrived.

He took his two gifts and thanked everyone. Good wishes were expressed all round. Mira smiled shyly at him. The two brothers shook his hand in the limp way of children. Mrs Singh thanked him for what he'd brought and he in turn thanked her, waving his packages. Mr Singh expressed the hope that Fergus would come to their home again soon.

As soon as he was back in his flat, Fergus tore off the wrapping paper. His presents were a set of vodka miniatures and a packet of panatellas. He smoked one before he went to bed and drank a sweet, strawberry-tasting vodka.

26

The Christmas tree was in the bay window decorated with fairy lights and coloured globes of glass which hung on golden thread.

On top was the cardboard king which he had made at nursery with its cotton wool beard and felt boots. Fergus was standing by the black slate mantelpiece — it had cards along the top — with his back to the round mirror. He could feel the flames of the turf fire on the backs of his legs. It was the Saturday before Christmas and he had arrived home the day before. He was drinking a whisky with ice and talking to his uncle Peter, his father's only brother.

'The thing with shock is that very often you don't feel it until some months, even years after the event,' said the older man.

Uncle Peter had iron-grey hair and bony hands. The edges of his tweed jacket were taped with leather to prevent fraying. Had his uncle worn the jacket when he had been at Hadley? Fergus wondered. It seemed familiar but then it was his uncle's style.

'Marjorie was telling me . . . .'

Uncle Peter waved towards his wife on the sofa talking to Pippa. The Christmas tree was behind them and light from the coloured bulbs showed here and there on the two figures.

'. . . about this young boy from Hong Kong called Hughes who's been with us for a couple of years and last year lost his mother . . . .'

As the wife of a housemaster, Fergus knew it often fell to Marjorie to look after boys in such predicaments at Hadley.

'At first he was tearful and depressed. Then he seemed to get over it. We all, and Marjorie in particular, heaved a great sigh of relief. But then the really strange thing started. He became obsessed with washing his hands. Couldn't stop doing it. Did it so much they went red and finally started to bleed. We sent him to a shrink and under hypnosis it emerged that this young boy . . . now, let me get it right . . . because he touched his mother in the coffin . . . Yes, this is right . . . got it into his head that he'd been the one who'd killed her. The washing of his hands was a symptom of wanting to renounce the stain of course, but also, and more importantly, according to the psychiatrist, the way he signalled to the world that he needed help. It wasn't just a symptom. It was attention-seeking. Which only goes to prove the human mind is a very strange place.'

Fergus nodded agreement. It was the way his uncle passed on old ideas as new and novel that especially tried his patience.

'What about you Fergus? How have you been coping?'

Now his uncle was asking him how he was. He should have seen

91

it coming, he told himself. That way he could have got something prepared.

'I haven't wanted to wash my hands,' he replied.

His uncle stared at him with unblinking grey eyes. No, he wasn't going to get away with being light.

He cleared his throat.

'Well . . . .'

He could sense Pippa on the sofa had fallen silent and was waiting for him to speak. He knew the answer to the question — that wasn't the problem. The stages flashed across his thoughts. After the beach he'd been shocked and incredulous. He couldn't believe what had happened. He'd kept thinking it would end like a bad dream although the quiet small voice said it wouldn't. After the reading of the will there'd been thoughts of revenge. That had been the time too of cruelty to his mother. Then had come the move to London and the quite unforeseen development; the growing feeling that he'd done such wrong as to deserve being passed over. With Pippa listening and his uncle, who'd once been one of his teachers, also listening, how did he explain his changing responses and their strange cumulation?

'I cry,' he said, 'when I'm alone.'

Pippa made a clicking sound of disapproval with her tongue. He turned his gaze from his uncle, who was looking at him with his head lolling sideways, to the sofa where Marjorie sat looking down at her hands and Pippa sat with her back to him.

'Did you say something Pippa?' he asked.

'Nothing.'

'I thought I heard you say something.'

Marjorie looked up and shook her head at him implying he should stop. She had watery blue eyes and long golden hair which was pinned at the back. His uncle squeezed his shoulder. But why should he be silent?

'If you've got something to say Pippa, why don't you get it off your chest?'

'Now, now,' Uncle Peter intoned, turning him by his shoulders back towards the fireplace. His mother and Dan, her brother, and Dan's wife, were looking at him from the other side of the room.

It was as if everyone was in on a secret except him. He hated this feeling of conspiracy. His uncle spoke. The sounds of conversation started in the room again. His outburst was apparently forgotten. After some moments he said he had to go out to the kitchen; he had to help with the preparations.

In the kitchen he found Dorothy. She was an old friend of his mother's, a woman in her early fifties. She had no family and by tradition came to them every Christmas and was an honorary aunt. She had thick calves and knees which seemed to lean towards each other. She was scraping carrots by the sink. He watched her running the peeler along the red stems, the thin lengths of skin coming away and falling onto other peelings tumbled together like straws in the game of Spillikins.

'What can I do?' he finally asked.

Pointing to the ham and the chicken on the table, she asked him to carve.

He drew out of the kitchen drawer the long carving knife which his father had wielded every Sunday and the X-shaped sharpener. The blade went into the crease. Schut, schut, schut, it ran up and down. Every time the tip neared the end his muscles tensed lest it should slip out and cut him and so it didn't get properly sharpened. The job finished, he ran his finger along and could feel the point wasn't as keen as the rest. This annoyed him.

The door opened and Pippa came in.

'Let me help,' she said, and Dorothy asked her to put the cress on the sandwiches.

Fergus put the carving fork with the yellowing ivory handle into the ham and began to slice sideways. Pippa, with giant scissors, was carefully cutting cress and scattering it. Dorothy with her peeler scraped away. The clock ticked. There was an oppressive atmosphere of silence. He could feel it pressing down on him, palpable, like damp. If you don't do something, he told himself, it will be another lost opportunity, and the distance between brother and sister will widen another couple of inches.

'How's life?' Fergus asked in a friendly way. It seemed like a good way to start. She could either tell him about her journey from Galway which she had made that afternoon or she could talk more generally.

'As well as can be expected,' she said which was not what he had in mind at all.

Dorothy dropped the carrots into a saucepan pitted with age and turned on the tap. The pipes rattled and water spurted.

'How was your train journey?' Dorothy asked.

'I had to stand all the way to Athlone,' came back Pippa's frosty reply.

Dorothy turned and rubbed the side of her nose with her wrist, presumably because her hands were wet.

'Your dress is lovely, I forgot to compliment you on it earlier.'

'It's rather heavy, Dorothy. It was made for the days when people lived with draughts. I bought it second-hand.'

It was velvet with a clasp at the front. Here now was his chance.

'Weren't you terribly hot inside?' he asked. 'I was standing by the fire and I was very hot.'

'I didn't feel the heat,' she said. She was looking down, no longer scissoring. 'I was thinking about other things. When something's weighing on one's mind one tends not to notice one's environment.'

An alarm sounded distantly at the back of his thoughts. The clock ticked. The saucepan filled with carrots and water banged onto the stove. Dorothy salted them. Fergus reminded himself to keep calm. The purpose of the conversation was that they make friends, not drive themselves further apart. He could pretend he hadn't heard, it hadn't happened. He could ask her what she'd bought him for Christmas, in a jokey sort of way. But then he thought, why should I? Her words were still with him. They had lodged in him like a barb. 'I was thinking about something else.' Well what bloody else? he wondered.

'What were you thinking about?' he asked.

Dorothy had the hard-boiled eggs by the sink. The tap splattered. She rapped one smartly against the side and pieces fluttered down onto the porcelain.

'I wouldn't like to say.'

She wouldn't like to say. She muttered the words in a tone of humble modesty which was apparently unaggressive — or would have seemed so to any listener — but which, to his acclimatised ear, was redolent with reproach and antagonism. Their arguments had always begun like this.

'Well you've started, so you might as well finish,' he said. He spoke slightly more loudly and considerably more curtly than usual. He may not have got angrier more quickly than she did but he certainly showed it sooner than she.

She was cutting again. The dark blades went through the anaemic cress stalks and white tubes tumbled down.

Why wasn't she replying? How did she think she could get away with something as insulting as pretending not to hear? He could feel his anger rising. At the same time he felt weary. It was all so familiar. Only an hour together and they were already back into the old pattern. He could see what was coming — oh yes, he knew exactly . . . .

She would remain silent. He would be first to shout. Then she would shout back. Then they would quieten down. Then she would say he'd started it because he'd been the one to shout first. Then he'd try to explain he'd shouted to get a reaction out of her. To which she'd reply, much like his father would have — his father used the same strategy in arguments and she wasn't his daughter for nothing — then she'd reply that shouting was possibly the worst way to get a reaction. Moreover it showed a lack of subtlety in thinking and a marked lack of consideration. Then Fergus would repeat, loudly this time, that he had to shout to get anywhere with her. Then she'd say he was shouting again. Then he'd say she was shouting too. She'd say she had no alternative but to shout; it was the only way to deal with a madman like himself. Then she'd leave the room and a few minutes later he'd hear the front door slamming, and she'd be off on one of her long walks from which she would return silent, superior and unapproachable. The pattern, established in childhood and perfected in adolescence, had not changed for years.

An entire shell came off an egg and fell into the sink, Fergus could feel his heart sinking. He could see it coming and it would be wonderful to step out of it. But he also recognised he'd got onto the moving train, so to speak, and now he couldn't get off.

'What was it you were thinking about?' he said. 'And don't bloody pretend you haven't heard my question this time.'

'Do I hear a raised voice?' said Dorothy.

Pippa said, 'You've got a lot to answer for.'

He had a lot to answer for. Such as what? Leaving his course? Taking his father to the beach and watching him dying? The thought crossed his mind that Pippa probably thought that he'd helped to push his father under.

'Jesus Christ, Pippa, do you ever let up?'

'Children,' Dorothy's voice wobbled slightly as if she was frightened. 'This is Christmas, not a time for argument.'

'Oh Dorothy . . .' he began but he couldn't imagine how he

would say to her this was their business and she should leave them be.

He turned back to Pippa and continued.

'You know, I would have thought, just this once, that you would have passed up the opportunity of trying to make me seem small and yourself seem bigger in comparison. But you couldn't, could you? You just can't.'

He began to carve furiously, pressing the knife through the flesh as hard as he could.

'Any opportunity for a dig, you'll take it. I started our conversation wanting to be friendly. But did you? Oh no! You wanted to argue. It's not enough for you to have been left everything? It's not enough for you to be the one who's going to finish her course, living up to the Maguire tradition of always finishing what they start, is it? No, you've got to have more, and the more you want is to make me feel this small.'

He held the fork and knife close together in the air.

'What do you think I feel? What do you think it's like living with the knowledge that your own father not only didn't approve but really didn't like you? It's fine for you. You've got ample proof of his love. But all I've got is the knowledge that he didn't at the end care for me and because he's dead I can't ask him to change his mind, explain, or make friends with him again. You try living with that, Miss High and Mighty, and you won't find it so very easy. Probably distinctly unpleasant. Unnerving. Undermining. Distressing. You do know what these adjectives mean, don't you? Don't they have that clinical feel to them that's your particular *métier*? Pippa, did you hear me? I'm talking to you . . . .'

Her little face creased up and tears started to roll down her cheeks. The scissors fell from her grasp, clattering on the table. She put her hands over her eyes.

'So what does it mean? "You've got a lot to answer for?"' He pronounced the sentence in an imitation girlish voice. 'You think it's all my fault. I decided not to continue my course of studies and so shortened the poor old man's lifespan? Or maybe you think I did it? Crept up from behind and dragged him under the waves.'

She started to sob.

'Is that what you meant?' he continued. 'In the light of your silence I can only presume. Come on Pippa. "You've got a lot to answer for." You said it. Now you explain it.'

The door opened and his mother came in. Her face was flushed.

'Leave her alone, for God's sake,' she said. 'I just heard what you said as I came down the corridor. It was disgusting. I want you to apologise at once. And to carry on like this in front of Dorothy as well. In that respect, it's the two of you who ought to be ashamed of yourselves.'

'Mother, Pippa just implied something about me which you didn't hear which was also disgusting,' said Fergus.

His mother looked at him.

'Fergus,' she said quietly. 'I want you to apologise.'

'We're grown-ups, Mother, Pippa and I, and sometimes we behave like them. You can't come in and tell us what to do like you used to do when we were children.'

These words came out without his expecting them. They surprised him. He didn't think he was capable of telling his mother to leave them be in such a way. As he grasped this he suddenly had a sense of drawing back and seeing himself in the kitchen at the table, carving; Pippa on the other side; his mother by the door; and in the living room at the front of the house, all his relatives. Peter would be standing with his back to the fire where Fergus had left him. Marjorie would be on the sofa with her head bent forward, turning the ice in her empty glass as she always did when she was nervous. Uncle Dan and Auntie May would be staring resolutely ahead, like a middle-aged couple on a Sunday afternoon sitting in a parked car. They would all be listening.

'Stop it now,' his mother shouted, 'and apologise.' Her hands trembled in front of her mouth as if she was about to be sick.

'Pippa has just insulted me.' Fergus spoke more quietly. He tugged at a clove buried in the fat, and when it wouldn't come began to lever at it with the end of his knife, his finger near the point.

'We're all just a bit overwrought,' said Pippa softly.

Overwrought. The sense of calm and drawing back disappeared as suddenly as it had come. As Dorothy dropped a kettle onto the stove he began to shout.

'Pippa, we're not overwrought. You have just accused me of causing Dad's death and we're having an argument about it. I, for some reason you don't seem to be able to comprehend, don't take well to your inference.'

'I didn't accuse you of any such thing,' she shouted back. 'I just said you had a lot to answer for.'

'No, you wouldn't accuse me of anything outright, face to face. But you and I know that's what you mean,' he shouted back.

He felt a slicing feeling in his fingers and let out a sharp, short shriek.

Three faces with slightly open mouths looked at him from different parts of the kitchen. His gaze lowered. Trying to remove the clove, he'd cut into his index finger. The wound was long and deep. Blood was already rising from the gouge, forming a shape like a billowing sail. Lifting his finger, red spattered down onto the meat below. He put his finger into his mouth. The blood tasted of iron.

A tea towel with 'Irish Linen' printed on it was wrapped around his finger.

'I'll dress it for you,' said Dorothy and went off to the medicine cabinet.

Pippa said, 'I still say we're overwrought.'

Maybe they were, he thought. Suddenly he didn't care any more. He thought of his childhood eyes, the ones out in space that gazed down without blinking. What could they possibly be making of it? In the course of his life the previous ten minutes were among the most unedifying. The eyes would surely count them against him and in his book of deeds they would be a black mark. His sister hadn't really accused him of killing his father. If he was really honest with himself he knew that. 'You've got a lot to answer for' had been her words, meaning, he presumed, 'You broke his heart.' As the towel stained red; as Pippa cut again with her scissors; and as his mother stared at him with an expression of hurt and anger, he could see all this only too clearly. And yes, maybe they were overwrought. Or maybe just he was. He had a sense of rising above and looking down on the situation. It was like being on a mountain top and seeing the clouds of a storm far below. He felt guilty too and he felt a nagging desire to propitiate the gaze and redeem himself.

'I'm sure we're overwrought,' he said slowly and wearily. He stared at his finger. His blood leaking through made the weave in the cotton stand out.

'Please, please children,' said their mother, 'no more quarrelling and tell me you're made up.'

Pippa and Fergus muttered their agreement as Dorothy returned with a bottle of disinfectant and a box of plasters.

Half an hour later came the delivery of a huge bunch of flowers from Jennifer which mollified his feelings.

27

Fergus sat on Laura's sofa. Her flat smelt vaguely of gas. The windows rattled in their casements and outside he could see a ragged square filled with bare leafless trees. Grey bark, darkening sky.

'How was your Christmas?' she asked. She was bending over the gas fire. It caught, making an alarming sound.

'How was my Christmas?' he said. 'Not so hot.'

'Family rows?'

'When are there not family rows? I think Christmas should be abolished. Or perhaps it could be staggered. Initials A to E one year, F to L the next and so on. Like the telephone directories. Then you'd only have to do it once every four years.'

Laura was showing him the cover of a glossy magazine.

'Have you seen this?'

He hadn't. He shook his head.

'This is what I had to welcome in the New Year. I'm furious.'

She bent the spine back and handed it to him.

It was a social page with various black-and-white photographs of ball-goers and couples at parties, and prominent in the middle was a photograph of Laura on the night in the Sacred Heart. It had been taken just after the moment when she had emptied the glass of Perrier over Jennifer. The background to the picture, the dining room of the Sacred Heart with its tables and chairs somehow accentuated the fact that she wasn't wearing any clothes. The caption underneath read, 'Laura Shellgate gets 'em off!'

'Oh Christ!' he said. Over the preceding months he'd forgotten about the evening. Now with the photograph it came back. Was some bad luck connected with the night trailing behind? he wondered.

'It's more than "Oh Christ!", Fergus. My stepmother was in the hairdressers when she came across it. That evening she rang me. "Darling . . . ."' Laura imitated Mrs Shellgate's ringing tones. '"I don't know if you know about this but there's a girlie photograph of you in this month's Social-Personal . . . ."'

'Who took it?'

'Sitting at the other end?'

He remembered now, the silver cases under the chairs.

'One of them works for this rag. I think she's called Braden something or other.'

'A girl?'

Laura nodded.

'I don't know. It could have been any of them. They're all bastards.'

She took the magazine from him and slid it behind a cushion where it was out of sight.

'Have I made a complete fool of myself?' she asked. 'You're my first boyfriend, and you owe it to me to tell the truth.'

Her appeal was sincere.

'I wouldn't say you didn't draw attention to yourself, but you didn't make a fool of yourself either.'

She squeezed his hand.

'I thought you were splendid and they only published that photograph because they envy you. Mean little shits.'

'Don't go on,' she said, 'you'll spoil it.'

Outside it began to rain, droplets splattering on the glass. The gas fire hissed. The sound of car doors banging sounded in the street. A winter's evening, cold and cheerless. They decided to fetch a take-away and watch a movie on TV.

28

Fergus stamped through Shepherd's Bush Market carrying a plastic bag filled with vegetables and two pieces of haddock wrapped in newsprint. Bright lengths of fabric hung in the shops and stalls on either side and everywhere, it seemed to him, there were clusters of women buying lengths while their children pulled on their arms or sat freezing in buggies with running noses.

Ahead of him, Fergus could see the Uxbridge Road and he accelerated through the crowds towards the relatively empty pavement. Jennifer would be at number twelve Mafeking House in half an hour.

'Get it now,' shouted a voice grimly, '*Right Forward*,' and Fergus saw, on the corner, holding a sheaf of newspapers against his stomach, a young man.

He stopped for a moment. There was something familiar about the face with the faint red patches under the skin and the short dark hair.

'Only twenty pence and your money goes to a good cause. You, sir, buy your copy of *Right Forward*.'

As Fergus registered the remark was addressed to him, he realised it was the young man who had come to enquire about his relations with his neighbours and then run away. From the way he had just been addressed, Fergus could tell the recognition wasn't mutual.

He took a coin out of his wallet and bought a copy, stopping there to look at it. It was an eight-page tabloid printed on coarse paper. 'Colour Quotas in Met.' was the headline on the lead story. The article, based on purportedly leaked documents, claimed the Home Office was going to make the force have one black policeman in four. Britain would sink into an African nightmare. Bribery would become the norm. The coloureds would favour their own and treat the whites doubly harshly, went the editorial printed in thick large letters on the centre pages. There were other topics covered in the paper: how to weed out those who scrounged on the welfare system; how to recognise malingerers and backsliders in the Tory party; the truth about South African democracy; and the conspiracy to make contraceptives available to the young.

After some moments reading, Fergus felt he had the measure of *Right Forward*. Turning round so the vendor could see him, he tore it in quarters and rammed the pieces down into a 'We're Working for a Cleaner City' bin filled with chip papers.

The youth, who saw what he had done, now turned away, and for the first time Fergus saw two older men were standing watching from a few yards up the road. They stared at him coldly and he judged they were minding the newspaper seller.

Shaking his head and scowling so his reaction could be clearly seen, he picked up his carrier filled with food and headed down the road, passing two Sikhs who were carrying cardboard boxes filled with ties.

29

A chrome bar ran diagonally across the door to the restaurant. Fergus pushed and stepped inside. Only a couple of tables were occupied.

'*Buon giorno*,' said the waiter, rubbing his hands. He was a square man with an enormous head. He wore a short maroon-coloured jacket.

'Anyone you want, sir?' He was smiling, revealing a gold tooth.

Fergus went to the table at the back near the Gaggia machine with its handles like beer pumps. He liked the smell of coffee.

The waiter undid the bottom button of his jacket. Fergus hung his coat on a peg and sat down. He picked up the menu. The waiter hovered beside him with notebook and pen. Fergus ordered pasta of the day which was spaghetti alle vongole, a glass of red wine and a roll and butter. The man went behind the counter and shouted in Italian down the dumb-waiter. A moment or two later the wine was put down in front of Fergus, along with the bottle for refills if he should want them. Fergus said, 'Thank you,' and sat back in his seat.

The window at the end of the restaurant was silvery from the light outside. He could see the dark shapes of the passers-by walking up and down. He took a small drink of wine and drew the letter out of his pocket. It had come just as he had been leaving for work and all morning he had kept reaching into his pocket and touching it to assure himself it was there. Now at last the moment had arrived; he was free to read it, slowly and with attention.

He turned it over and read his mother's address on the back. Her writing was pointed like every old person's seemed to be. She had used a biro.

He drew the letter out. It was written on several sheets of blue Basildon Bond paper. He folded it back and began to read:

Jan 19th

Dearest Fergus,

Oh my darling. What a long way you are from home and how little you write to me. You are in my thoughts all the time. I think of you when I wake up in the morning and all through the day and last thing at night when I am waiting to fall asleep. I even dream of you: sometimes as a small baby, your skin all red and tears streaming down your cheeks; or sometimes as an infant, in your shorts and the plastic Roman helmet which you loved, running around the garden with the wooden sword which Uncle Peter made you; or sometimes as an adolescent, sitting silently at the bottom of the hall stairs with your packed bags beside you, waiting to go back to school; or finally as you are now. My darling Fergus, I cannot tell you how much I miss you and how much I worry about you now that you are so far, far from home.

And I think, my dear, I can understand what has made you leave. As far back as I can remember, you have always had the feeling that Pippa was preferred to you. Especially by your father. Then your father died and there was the will and that was the proof that it was so. This is how it seems from your

103

point of view. But oh my darling Fergus, you were never loved less than your sister. It was always equal. Your father and I loved you both the same, never preferring one over the other, and never not giving to one what we gave to the other. I promise you this on my heart and you must believe it is so. Ever since you asked me at Christmas, when we had that long talk about you and Pippa, if she was preferred to you, I have been racking my brains to think of a single instance when this was so, a single instance which would support what you believe, and I can't think of one.

But of course, I can hear you saying, even as I write here in the kitchen with the clock ticking on the wall, what about the will? Well, Fergus, it's time to be honest. You did upset your father. You weren't happy at school or at university and then you went away to London for the whole summer term without telling us and then the university told you to leave. It did upset your father tremendously. He could not understand how you could just absent yourself without telling anyone — it seemed so careless, Fergus, and so unthinking. Nor could he understand that you didn't want to finish your course. However this won't come as a surprise to you, given what his family believe about finishing whatever they start. He was angry darling, for very good reasons, and he acted rashly. But I don't believe — and I say this having searched my heart long and hard — I don't believe he would have left the will as it was, if he had lived longer. He would have changed it back so that you and Pipps would get an equal share of what there was. I know he would. I promise you. He just did what he did because he was angry; and haven't we all acted rashly when we've been angry? Had he lived, his anger would have worn off. He would have made friends with you again, (— I know he'd be so proud if he could see you now working in London —), he would have seen that his decision was petty-minded and pointless, and he would have changed the will back again. These aren't the rantings of an old woman. I know they are true. Please, please, believe and please, most important of all, forgive and forget: write to Pippa; and tell yourself that in spite of everything, you love your father. If we keep our hearts hardened for too long, we stop being people and turn into rocks and you're too good for that and far too talented my darling.

The waiter put the plate of food down on the table, a fork and spoon wrapped in a serviette and the roll and butter. Fergus waited until he was gone and then read on:

We had a terrible storm last Saturday. The windows rattled all night in their frames and four slates came off the roof. Some water got in and the ceiling of the back bedroom was stained brown as a result. I had to get a man in to do repairs. He charged me £25.00 just for bringing a ladder and going up on the roof for ten minutes. I think workmen think that if you're a woman alone, they can ask the earth and get away with it.

The days here are long, the nights are longer, and the house seems so empty without your father moving about. I miss the way he would have the radio on, the distant sound of him hammering in the garage, the way he would whistle through his teeth when he went about his odd jobs.

Pippa wrote — I had a letter from her only a couple of days ago. She's moved to a new house in Salthill which she's sharing with three other girls. She gets a room to herself and she likes it very much. The course is apparently so-so, but she's determined to see it out to the bitter end, she says, so she can write BA after her name. (She's definitely a Maguire in that sense.) Next time she comes she's bringing a young man with her to meet me. He's called Michael — not a student — he works in the building business. We haven't talked about what happened at all, or the rights and wrongs of it but when she's here we will, please God, and I shall tell her very plainly that the will we heard wasn't really your father's decision and we must face facts and think what his real intentions were. She's a good girl. I'm sure she'll see sense.

Fergus darling, come home soon, even if only for a weekend. I want to see you and have you here in the house and hear every bit of news that you have. And please write soon my darling. I miss you very much.

With all my love,
Mam

Attached to the last sheet with a paper clip was a blue twenty-pound note with a map of the Aran Isles drawn in grey on the front. Fergus put it in his wallet.

'Excuse me, I'm sorry to disturb you.'

Fergus heard the softly spoken words with dread. He looked up and saw the speaker was Mr Wiggins. He was standing nearby, holding his briefcase with both hands.

'Oh,' said Fergus sullenly.

'I didn't mean to startle you.'

Fergus flattened out the letter and re-folded it, using the handle of the fork to iron down the creases.

'I was sitting in the corner having a bite, and I couldn't help noticing you.'

Fergus nodded, put his fork into his vongole and began to twist.

'May I sit down and join you?'

'This is my lunch hour. I'm not at work and I would like to be left alone.'

'I understand. I absolutely respect what you're saying. I'm terribly sorry for barging in. Excuse me.'

Mr Wiggins performed a little bow, walked back along the length of the restaurant and took the seat that was diagonally opposite Fergus.

'Coffee,' called Mr Wiggins, giving a little wave to the waiter.

Fergus broke open the roll and covered half of it with cold butter which did not spread evenly. As he chewed he felt the desire growing to see what Mr Wiggins was doing, until he was not able to think about anything else. It was like having an itch which was growing stronger and stronger.

The door of the restaurant banged shut. The noise broke Fergus' concentration. Before he knew what he was doing he looked and saw Wiggins was still in his seat. The older man smiled in response and offered a little salutation with his coffee cup. Fergus pretended not to see and looked back down at his plate with a scowl. There was grit in one of the clams which crunched between his teeth. He pushed the dish away. He wanted to hit Mr Wiggins. How dare the man accost him at lunchtime. He remembered Sharon, talking cheerfully to him. She too deserved blame for what was happening. Finally, there was Martin-Smith, who had turned *The Torture Papers* in that irritating way with the end of his pen and who had failed to mention the matter of Mr Wiggins to Fergus in advance. He wanted to shout at them all.

'You do not like?' The waiter was standing over Fergus with a sorry look on his face.

'I'm not hungry.'

The waiter turned his mouth down at the edges.

'Something else?'

'The bill.'

The waiter hurried off. Fergus pressed his hand on the table top. When he lifted it away a misty imprint of condensation was left behind.

'How was your dinner? It's very good here, wouldn't you say?'

Mr Wiggins got up from his table as Fergus opened the door onto the street.

'It was fine.'

'I noticed you sent some back.'

Fergus nodded curtly and stepped outside.

'Do you mind if I walk with you?'

Mr Wiggins had his head through the doorway.

Fergus made no response and started in the direction of the office. The pavements were crowded but the roads were empty and the air was filled with the eerie sound of footfalls. After a few seconds he sensed that Mr Wiggins, having caught up with him, was at his side.

'I like that place a lot,' he said. 'I think it's very good value. I use it whenever I'm in town.'

'Mr Wiggins. My lunchtime is my own time. I don't want to be disturbed with office business.'

Mr Wiggins began to swing his briefcase and to whistle *'Mademoiselle from Armenteers'* through his teeth. Stop it! Fergus wanted to shout.

Mr Wiggins broke off whistling and asked cheerfully, 'Have you read my book yet?'

Fergus sighed. 'Your book was sent, not to me, but as I explained, to another person in the company. It is for them to reply, not me.'

He tapped Fergus on the arm and repeatedly raised his eyebrows like a clown.

'It's pretty hot shit, isn't it?'

'Mr Wiggins, please leave me alone,' said Fergus.

Mr Wiggins said nothing. They walked on, side by side. At the entrance to the office block, Mr Wiggins opened the door and

Fergus stepped through. Jack was standing in his customary position against the wall smoking his pipe.

'Hello there, Jack,' Mr Wiggins called cheerily across the lobby.

'Hello, Charlie,' Jack called back.

With a sense of alarm Fergus realised that the two men were on speaking terms. He pressed the lift call button.

'If this is the young man you meant . . . ?' It was Jack speaking. 'You're in very good hands.'

'We're going to make a film out of my book, aren't we Fergus?' Mr Wiggins shouted to him from behind. Fergus touched the metallic doors of the lift, covered with grubby hand marks.

'But I don't have anything to do with the making of the programmes,' said Fergus. 'I'm in a different department.'

'We know that,' said Jack. 'But you're a clever lad. One day you will.'

Alone in the lift Fergus banged the metal walls with anger. When he went into reception he saw Sharon was standing on a chair, watering the potted plants that hung from cradles. He could not bring himself to talk to her and, before she could engage him in conversation, he turned down the corridor and escaped. Outside his own office door he paused for a moment. Please let Martin-Smith not be there, he recited. But he could hear faint rustling beyond the wood which augured badly. He pushed the door back and saw that, yes, his colleague was at his desk.

Martin-Smith had a napkin tucked into his collar and was sucking up Perrier water through a bendy straw from a small green bottle. Even when he was alone Martin-Smith's manner didn't change. In front of him there was a silver foil dish with a plastic spoon sticking out of it.

'Hello whipper-snapper,' said the older man, looking up.

'I forgot something,' said Fergus. He knew he couldn't possibly stay in the room.

Pointedly leaving the door open, he went over to his desk and pretended to get something out of one of his drawers.

'What are you eating?' he asked.

'Chicken korma.'

Fergus made a noise of disapproval.

'Too much for your frail little stomach? I suppose you only eat potatoes?'

'I'm such a raw nerve of sensitivity,' agreed Fergus, 'I don't eat at all.'

He closed the door after himself. No, he wasn't going to leave by the front entrance. Sharon would have finished watering the plants and would be sitting at her desk.

He went down the fire escape into the yard where they kept the OB vans and slipped through the side entrance into Bridle Lane.

30

Once outside he started to walk. He didn't have a clue where he was going. He went down to Brewer Street, turned right and found his way along to Regent Street. The pavements were crowded with pedestrians. The winter sales were on. A police-woman with a loudhailer stood on the corner.

'Wait by the kerb. Do not move,' she ordered.

Finally the traffic stopped. He crossed the road with a stream of people and went under the arch into Swallow Street. It was quieter here, less crowded. There were photographs of women in spangled costumes and the men in boleros, in the entrance of a club. He could hear the policewoman behind him issuing her instructions and sense the presence of the crowds. All those people thought of themselves as a centre, he supposed, as *the* centre. Even in the middle of crowds they forgot everyone else and thought of themselves in that way. It was a mistake he made as well.

Two policemen sauntered by, heading for Vine Street. He emerged onto Piccadilly and crossed onto the south side. The black railings of St James's church were hung with hand-made placards advertising lectures on Jung and Christianity, homo-sexuality and Jesus. He went through the imposing gateway and down wide, worn steps. In the church courtyard within, there was a market with covered stalls. The first stand was selling printers' blocks, the idea being to buy the two or three which made up one's initials. In the second there was Scottish knitwear.

Somewhere, scented candles were burning. A blonde woman in moonboots stamped her feet and blew onto her hands.

'It's a cold day to be standing around,' said Fergus.

'You're telling me, darling.'

He ambled around listlessly picking up goods, asking their prices without interest, putting them back. He was brooding on his mother, his sister, his family, growing angry and despondent. Why did these thoughts never leave him alone? Why too was it always the old wearisome pattern of fury and self-pity?

He left the stall where he had been browsing through a box of old etchings and made his way to the small green which lay to the side of the church. Here there were four or five empty, pigeon-coloured benches, walks flagged with York stone, and small lawns with grey earth showing through at the edges because it was winter.

He sat down. It didn't feel quite as cold as it had been that morning.

He told himself the observation was banal and wished he could stop what was pressing at the back of his mind.

He looked up. The sky was a sort of dark pearly colour and there was a stillness which he connected with the onset of snow. He thought with pleasure of the snow flakes floating down but nothing was going to be strong enough or engaging enough to stop what was coming. He could feel it, yes, closer and closer. There wasn't anything else to be done but to go with it.

He closed his eyes. He was back in the Dublin house. He was standing in the hall by the mahogany table, with the bronze nude resting on top. The front door was behind and the stairs stretched ahead to the landing window fringed with red glass. The walls were cream, the doors painted black, and the red Turkish carpet worn at the edges. He was himself as he was in London but he was also his younger, adolescent self. He could hear his father in the study twiddling with the dials of the radio. With measured steps he glided down the corridor, past the cupboard smelling of apples. He opened the study door.

'You didn't knock,' his father said, keeping his back to his son.

Fergus closed the door behind.

'There's something I wanted to ask you,' Fergus said.

The door clicked shut, the sound above all others which he connected to interviews in the study.

'Ask away. A question's always free. I've always said that. Just don't expect an answer.'

His father was sitting at the octagonal cane table on which the radio lived. The arm behind the wave guide was sliding like an upright needle, backwards and forwards. Where the paint on the guide had worn thin over the years, the valves inside showed through, glowing white and orange. From the speaker a cacophony of sounds cackled out, snatches of music and the human voice, mixed with other, unidentifiable hisses and whispers.

'I wanted to ask about that. Do you remember when you fixed it?'

Fergus pointed to the right-hand pane of the bow window at the end of the cluttered room. There was a nut attached to a bolt running through the glass. Outside the hilly garden rose and fell to brambles and in the distance lay the grey Irish Sea.

His father looked up for a moment and then went back to the radio.

'What are you talking about?' he asked sarcastically.

Fergus opened his mouth and quite unexpectedly started to speak much more loudly than he had ever spoken in his father's presence before.

'You have never listened to me properly in my entire life,' he bellowed, 'so I wonder if you could manage it just this once?'

His thighs were trembling just as they might have done before a fight at school. His father turned and looked at him sourly.

'So this is *the* adolescent rebellion?' he said, 'the one we read about in books. Dr Spock and all that codswallop.'

Do not answer the question. The thought formed in Fergus' mind. It was simple and emphatic. He could see his father was staring at him with dark eyes. He gauged the expression was a mixture of anger and disgust. He lifted his gaze to the window. The announcer mentioned something about a Sibelius symphony.

'Don't get hysterical Fergus,' his father said coldly. 'Remember, we're civilised human beings. We're not in the caves any more, shouting and throwing spears. We signal to one another with something called language. Yes, I do remember when I fixed the window. Extremely clearly as it so happens.'

'So do I,' said Fergus. 'What I remember is that I was with Pippa. We were playing in the garden together, throwing stones

111

onto the roof and watching them clatter down the tiles. One of the stones wasn't aimed properly. It hit the window and the glass cracked. You came out and shouted at us.'

His father leant back in the cane chair covered with the Turkish rug. He folded his hands over his stomach and nodded. Fergus felt his courage might desert him but it was too late to go back. He started again, breathlessly:

'As a punishment you made us stand and wait while you fetched your tools from the garage. Then we had to watch while you fixed the pane. You took hours finding the right sized bolt, filing down the end so there wasn't a stub sticking out, then rethreading it and finally putting it in place with the big washers on either end which would hold the glass. When it was over you said to Pippa that she could go but you said that I had to stay for another hour because I had thrown the stone. It was Pippa who threw the stone yet you blamed me, and that is how it's always been from the beginning to now. I've been the one who's always done wrong. Pained my mother, offended our relatives, behaved "gracelessly". . . .'

'Oh, Fergus,' his father interrupted. 'You're over-reacting as usual. You surely can't be trying to make out a case based on the example of a broken window. . . .'

Here, the reverie foundered. They always seemed to do this before they were satisfactorily resolved. The study started to fade, and with it went the sound of the symphony drifting from the wireless, the smell of lanolin which his father rubbed on his hands morning and night to stop them chafing, and all the other physical details. Then his father himself began to recede and finally Fergus was left alone in a clean white space.

'Why have you never forgiven me anything? Why have I no happy memories of us together? — which must be a record. Why have you never in your life once lifted a finger to help me . . . ?'

The words stopped. His mind felt like a blade in a sawmill, which, having no wood to cut on, turned uselessly, wildly. The worst of it was there was nothing to be done with the mind in that state. He knew this from experience. It would just have to be left until it settled back to what it had been.

He sensed something cold on his eyelid. He began to open the lid and felt that it was obstructed. He put his finger to the place and felt wet. Of course, while he'd been stting there, brooding, it had started.

He opened his eyes. The snow was coming down in small pieces which reminded him of rice. He felt a surge of expectation and an indefinable but powerful sense of excitement, which the first moments of snow had always brought on from as far back as he could remember.

He looked up. For as far as he could see the sky was filled with tiny little fluttering pieces of white moving against a grey background. He could feel a settling, the agitation of a few moments before going, a coming sense of peace. And all that had been required, it seemed, to set the change in motion was a simple event, the falling of snow. In an unfocused way he thought about how quickly his mind could change.

He leant back in his seat to observe. The snow began to come more quickly, the flakes to increase in size. He watched the ground. First the flakes were only dots of white on the stones, the grass and the benches. Then they were joined by other flakes. Slowly islands formed. The islands grew bigger until the spaces between the islands filled and suddenly it was as if a thin white blanket had been laid down. He sat quite still as he watched, letting the snow fall on his outstretched arms which lay along the back of the bench until they too were covered. A simple fall of snow and his feelings started to change. As the snow began to accumulate, thickening the blanket and obscuring the faint hue of colour from the lawns, benches and stones beneath, he pondered this. There was a lesson here that he had to learn, and if he didn't, he thought, he'd never escape from his preoccupations. There was a world outside himself, alive and vigorous, as against the world of within, and he had to go out to it. He had to stop thinking and leap and if he could, he knew he would find undreamt of and unexpected consolations.

The snow was thick on the ground. He stood up and shook himself. Little flurries fell away from his sleeves and his shoulders. On the bare patch on the bench where he had been sitting, flakes were already beginning to alight.

He started to walk back towards the market. Snow crunched underfoot. At the top of the steps which led out of the garden, he turned and looked back. He had been lucky to have had the whole place to himself, he thought. He let his eye roam along his footprints. His place on the bench already had a fine dusting of flakes on it. In Piccadilly it wouldn't be settling, of course, and under

the wheels of the traffic the snow would be turning to slush. A
depressing thought. But in the little garden it had covered the
earth over and that was what he would picture on his way back to
the office: the courtyard, the benches, the lawns, all covered over
and his single set of footprints leading away.

He took a last look around the courtyard and headed for
Piccadilly.

31

Jennifer lay in the bed closest to the wall, her hair fanned out on
the pillow. Fergus was on his side next to her. He ran his hand up
the inside of her thighs to her sex and then down towards her
knees again. At the same time they kissed tentatively with only
the tips of their tongues touching.

Jennifer turned her head away. Her legs opened under the bed-
clothes and her pelvis came forward to meet his hand as it came
up. Fergus opened his eyes. Jennifer's face was pale in the
darkness, her lids firmly closed, the expression one of expectation
and patience. He touched her lips with his tongue. What remained of her lipstick was sweet like confectionery. She opened
her mouth to reveal two rows of neat white teeth, whilst under the
covers she took his hand, pushed it against her groin and squeezed her legs. This was the only demonstrative action that she
regularly made in their love-making.

He took Jennifer's other hand and moistened her fingertips
with his saliva. Then they kissed whilst her hand went down the
bed and wet the end of his glans. It aroused him, the sensation of
her fingers ringed around him. He lifted himself onto his elbows
and dropped between her legs. She grasped his penis and pulled it
upwards. Their bodies pushed and pulled. They adjusted their
positions to each other. Suddenly he could feel from the warmth
that was clinging to him that he was in her.

He began to move the middle of his body inwards and outwards. Jennifer opened and widened. He felt the calloused edges of her heels resting on his calves. She sighed. He kissed her on the ear and smelt her hair. He remembered Jennifer's face as he had seen it on the pillow a moment before. He wet the end of a finger, leant onto his side and slid his hand between their bodies until it found the secret place right at the bottom of her belly. He began to rub and she sighed again. He pressed harder with his finger, and she started to run her fingernails up and down his spine. He felt her tongue touching the lobe of his ear and moving it back and forth.

Suddenly Jennifer rolled her head to the side. He lifted up his head and looked at her. She was wide-eyed.

'Did you hear that?'

'What?'

'Can't you hear it?'

He turned his head and listened. He could hear the curtains stirring as they were fanned by wind coming through the open window and, more distantly, the reassuring hum of the refrigerator beyond the kitchen wall.

'I don't hear anything,' he said. 'What am I meant to be hearing?'

The refrigerator clicked off. There was a hiatus of silence.

'It's a sort of wailing,' she said. 'Surely you can hear it?'

He angled his head again but heard nothing.

'It must have gone,' he said.

He started to kiss the side of her turned-away face.

'Come on, it's nothing.'

He cupped a hand over a breast and began to stroke it. She returned his kisses, opening her mouth and pressing her tongue against his. Fergus let his hand slide back down. As he found the spot, she stiffened and turned away from him.

'There it is again,' she said urgently.

This time Fergus could hear it. It was a faint and ominous wailing coming from the front of the flat.

'We must see what it is.'

Slowly he pulled himself out of her and got up. He found his trousers and a jumper on the chair. Leaning against the wall for balance, he pulled on a pair of slippers.

Jennifer was getting out of bed.

'I'm coming too,' she whispered. In the distance the wailing sounded more loudly.

He went to the front door and carefully turned the latch making a minimum of noise. Jennifer followed, bare-footed and swathed in his dressing gown.

The door swung open, the flap along the bottom rustling on the brown mat, and the night air blew in.

He went to the middle of the balcony and stopped. The moaning was quite audible now, rising and falling like wind in a chimney flue. It was coming from below.

He crept to the wall and leaned over, pressing his thighs on the cold brick. On the muddy grass underneath, eight or ten figures squatted on the ground around the Singhs' flat. They had their heads thrown back and were moaning like wolves.

Throw something, he thought. The family at the far end of the balcony had plants in pots outside their flat. But what if he hit one of them? His front door being the first at the top of the stairs, he would be the obvious suspect.

He put his fist against his mouth and blew. It had to be done without thinking.

He drew himself up and leaned over the parapet.

'Oi,' he shouted, swaying slightly to give the impression he had just woken up.

In the darkness below the heads rolled forward. There could be no going back.

'Some people are trying to sleep around here. So why don't you bugger off and play in the park.'

The moaning stopped. The night was quite still except for the faraway rumble of traffic on the motorway. He could sense every pair of staring eyes.

'Go on, fuck off the lot of you.'

'Maybe we should go back in,' whispered Jennifer from the doorway.

'Go on,' Fergus shouted down.

The pale faces were still angled towards him.

'Right, I'm going to 'phone the police.'

He turned away. From below came the blessed sound of movement. He counted five and looked over. They were all running. They moved in a bunch with a couple of the slower ones trailing behind to form a tail. Someone said something and they all laughed. At the corner they turned right and disappeared up Mafeking Road, the sound of their footfalls growing fainter and fainter until they merged into the traffic.

'I think I ought to go downstairs,' he said.

Jennifer pulled on a pair of old green wellingtons. He put the door decorated still with Kenny's pastoral landscape onto the latch. He led the way and she followed. He felt nervous now that the youths had run off; more nervous than when they had been there. He wanted to pee.

On the halfway landing he leaned around the corner. He expected something to be waiting at the bottom but there was nothing. Only the gloomy entrance lit up with a single bulb and the pathway to the pavement.

Jennifer found his hand on the cold metal bannister. They began to steal forward like children.

Nearing the bottom he saw. The paintwork and surrounding brickwork of the Singhs' front door were covered with red. He ran forward pulling Jennifer with him. At the bottom the light was weak. It was not until he got the half-metallic, half-sawdust smell that he realised. The door was covered with blood. Snaking from the letterbox hung a length of intestine like an obscene parody of a string of sausages. On the threshold there were trotters and several dark shapes which he guessed were offal. Inside the flat a child was crying. He rapped on the door and then wiped his knuckle on the brick.

'It's all right,' Jennifer called out. 'It's Fergus who lives upstairs.'

Chains clattered and bolts were drawn. The door opened and a pair of angry eyes looked out. It was Mr Singh's square brown face.

'Those bloody bastards.'

'They've gone now,' said Jennifer.

Someone began to sob. Mr Singh disappeared. Fergus counted five chains looping between the lintel and the door.

Mrs Singh appeared. She half-closed the door and undid the other chains. They clinked inside like a collection tray going round chapel.

The door swung back. Some of her hair had come away from her plait and was sticking out. In the kitchen behind, her husband was muttering to himself as he fetched something from

117

under the sink. There was a cigarette burning in the ashtray on the table.

The door swung back. She looked at its blood-covered surface blankly and then at the dark lumps scattered across the threshold. Mr Singh returned with a pair of tongs and a plastic bucket. Everyone stood back. The trotters dropped into the bucket with a hollow sound, followed by the heart with its dangling tubes. He went to pick up the liver but couldn't get a grip with the small rounds on the ends of the tongs. Mira brought him a salver and he worked the organ on with the edge of his shoe. It sprawled over the edges of the utensil as he moved it through the air and made an obscene sound as it joined the rest of the offal. With the brains and the other pieces he used the salver again. Finally, with a pair of scissors, Mr Singh cut the intestine from the letter-box and the length fell into the bucket held by him underneath like a collapsing rope. Then he went behind the door and when Mira pressed the flap, he caught the other half.

Mr Singh went back to the kitchen. Fergus watched as Mira held open a white plastic bag and he tipped everything into it. The bag was tied but inside the dark shapes of the offal could still be seen.

'Fergus got rid of those people,' said Jennifer.

Mrs Singh nodded and began to cry quietly. She bowed her head and wiped her eyes. Mr Singh said something in Hindi.

'Listen,' Fergus continued, 'if anything else happens, we're only a few feet away.'

'Get a broom and knock on the ceiling. We'll hear you upstairs,' Jennifer added.

Mrs Singh did not look up but nodded to show she had understood.

'I'm going to get the bastards,' shouted Mr Singh, 'I'm going to get them.' He was sitting in the kitchen drinking a Special Brew. Mira at the sink was rinsing the bucket.

'So, you understand, knock on the ceiling.'

'Yes,' Mrs Singh said, sounding as if she were angry with them. The door closed.

Fergus and Jennifer climbed the stairs silently, the sound of the re-engaging locks and chains fading behind them.

When they got back into bed Jennifer whispered, 'I love you.'

118

32

At Portobello Green, voices echoed off the Westway overhead and cars could be heard like distant water splashing. They hurried on, passing the stretch of clothes shops and a stall selling Jamaican hats and into the quietest section of the market by the walls of the convent. Here the stalls were loaded with incongruous items, old bakelite switches, battered shoes, warped forty-fives in grubby covers. A woman with swollen legs overturned her basket, spilling bruised and damaged vegetables which she had collected lower down the market. Fergus bent down to help her and she snarled at him, 'Fuck off,' so vehemently he almost toppled over. Jennifer linked arms with him as they walked off, and they laughed together.

A vendor wheeling a theatrical costume rack passed and they saw a small crowd gathered at the back of a grey van. They went up and saw a man in his fifties, with only one leg, prostrate on the ground, gleaming aluminium crutches on the filthy pavement beside him. The bag of laundered clothes which the one-legged man had been carrying had spilt its contents everywhere, and among the shirts and spotless white vests Fergus noticed half a dozen pairs of socks.

'What happened?' he asked.

The boy beside Fergus, who had white skin and a dirt mark on his cheek, looked at him blankly, turned and walked away, followed by two smaller boys. Three girls were left. The one in the middle had a small mouth and wore a Wuzzles tee-shirt. She looked up and said, 'My dad's gone for the ambulance.'

They all looked down. Was the man who was stretched out still breathing? Fergus looked at his face. It was long and sallow. Perhaps the man was dead, his body already growing cold? Fergus felt slightly nauseous. Jennifer touched the bottom of his back, first gently and then more forcibly, so that her intention could not be misunderstood.

He knelt. The man's eyelids weren't quite closed and a thin

119

strip of white could be seen. Suddenly Fergus imagined two eggs intead of eye sockets, the lids opening and the soft cooked yellow running out. He felt sick. Please, he pleaded inwardly, he did not want to touch the man.

He began to tear a strip out of his cheque book. He could feel the girls watching as he did this. They would never know his inspiration was fear.

He held the strip under the nose and it wavered.

'He's breathing,' said Fergus.

He picked up two shirts and a vest, which were on the pavement, gave them a shake and put them into the plastic bag with the rest of the laundry. The pairs of socks followed. The job done, he folded the top of the bag over and put it under the one-legged man's head.

'Here comes our dad,' said the girl in the Wuzzles tee-shirt.

Fergus stood up and a big pot-bellied man came over.

'I've called the ambulance,' he said crossly.

Everyone stood about not quite knowing what to do. Jennifer asked the pot-bellied man how long the ambulance would take and he began to talk. In his opinion, the collapse of the one-legged man and the length of time which the ambulance was taking, as well as the general deterioration of the market, were totally due to the cuts in government expenditure. Everything could be traced back to this evil. 'If they go on at this rate, soon there won't be anything left *to* cut,' he repeated endlessly, as if this were the ultimate refutation of government policy. Fergus and Jennifer listened, nodding now and again.

Just when he had decided they should leave, they heard the 'wh-wuh' of a siren and down the road came first a police car which cleared the crowds, its blue beacon flashing, and then behind it a white ambulance.

The two vehicles pulled up by the grey van. The ambulance men came over with a gleaming chrome stretcher covered with a red blanket. A policeman got out of the front of the maroon Vauxhall Cavalier, and then out of the back climbed a man in a suit whom Fergus recognised immediately as Curry. Within an instant, it flooded back effortlessly: the night in the Sacred Heart; the journey in the police car when the world had slid past the windows; Curry and himself in the interrogation room, sitting opposite each other at the table bolted to the floor. He remembered how frightened he had been, how disorientated and how unable to act, and the relief when Curry had announced he could go. Later, he had obsessively pondered why they had been let go. It hadn't made sense and at the back of his mind he'd sensed it wasn't by any means the end of the matter. With time that apprehension had slipped from his thoughts but now it was back, at the centre.

Curry was drawing closer, with his brown eyes and his big nose with the mark wiggling across the middle. He was a large man with a forceful stride. You've nothing to worry about, Fergus told himself. He had done nothing. Fergus nodded his head in greeting and Curry nodded in return.

'You got here very quickly,' he said.

Curry nodded. They watched the stretcher gliding through the air. The ambulance doors shut. One of the uniformed officers called over. Curry gestured, indicating that he was coming.

'I've had my eye on you, Mr Maguire,' he said mysteriously.

He stared with his impenetrable brown eyes. The mark on his nose was even more alarming than Fergus remembered. 'I've had my eye on you.' Fergus puzzled at the words but they did not make sense. 'I've had my eye on you, Mr Maguire . . . .'

'. . . And you've been a very good boy,' continued Curry.

The detective ducked away into the car. The beacon on the Cavalier's maroon roof whirled again and its blue light swirled against the brick walls of the convent. Fergus felt his heart starting to pump. 'I've had my eye on you, Mr Maguire, and you've been a very good boy.' Jennifer took his arm.

'What was that about?' she asked anxiously.

He shrugged his shoulders as if he didn't have an answer but his thoughts were racing. Perhaps the evening in the Sacred Heart was a curse that was going to follow him?

'I don't know,' he said and they walked on in silence. Near the Golborne Road he felt queasy and they went into a café to sit down. He felt he'd put his hand into a trap, and before he'd been able to get it out, it had shut.

121

33

It was midday on Saturday. Fergus was in the sitting room of Stoneleigh House playing backgammon with Henderson. It was the house of Hilary's mother and father and on the other side of the room sat Jennifer who was down for the weekend as well.

French windows stretched along one side of the room with a sodden lawn beyond and a ha-ha beyond that. In the fields further away were the dark shapes of cattle. The fire hissed and smoked in the grate.

'I think we all need cheering up.'

It was Hilary's father, a big, red-faced man. His head was around the door.

He disappeared before anyone could reply and returned with a bottle of sherry.

'Shall we have a drink?' he asked.

Fergus volunteered to fetch some glasses from the kitchen. When he got there, he found Hilary and her mother talking in low tones while leaning against the silver bar of the Aga.

'What do you want?' Mrs Lumley asked him very curtly as he came in. She was wearing a turtle-neck sweater which stretched tightly over her ample bosom.

'I've come to get some sherry glasses,' he explained.

'What a time to interrupt,' she said loudly, rushing across to the painted cabinet where the glasses were stored. 'And why can't you use your initiative and get them yourself?'

'Let me get them,' he said.

He stepped up but she turned her back to him. The width of her hips was exaggerated by the tightness of her ski-pants. So she was going to play that game. No, you can't help me. You're going to have to stand and watch while I do it *and* you're going to have to listen to me complain about it.

'Please let me get them,' he pleaded.

'I've started now.'

She lifted out the eggcup-shaped glasses two at a time and

slapped them down on the kitchen table making a great deal of noise.

'You're going to break them and then you'll be even crosser,' said Hilary quietly.

'Hilary, I have been ferrying glasses in and out of this cupboard since long before you were thought of, so please do me the courtesy of not telling me my business.'

'All right, nothing to do with me.'

Fergus circled the table so he could get at the cabinet on the other side of Mrs Lumley. But before he could start to help she shifted her body the other way, blocking him again.

'Tray,' Mrs Lumley bellowed.

Hilary handed one across. Fergus closed the cabinet doors and turned to look out of the window. Beyond the diamond shaped panes a line of yew trees stretched to a redbrick wall and, as he stared, impressions from the weekend passed across his thoughts. Arriving late at Henderson's flat on Friday evening and receiving a cold reception from his friend who was deaf to his explanation that his tube had stopped in a tunnel. A surprisingly quick journey through the northern suburbs of London to the A1, and all the while Hilary, much to his mystification, stroking Henderson on the back of his neck and Jennifer making faces at him when he looked puzzled. Arriving at Stoneleigh House, being brought into the living room, and suddenly realising Jennifer, Hilary and Henderson had slipped away to change, not having thought to take him with them, which left him with Mr and Mrs Lumley who he didn't know. Meeting the other guests: Hilary's brother, a tall etiolated young man called Andrew, and Bertie, who was drunk and failed to recognise him. Eating sausages and mash in the dining room on the Friday evening, while the labrador, Yummy, ate noisily from his bowl under the sideboard, with Mrs Lumley saying, 'Who's-a-good-boy?' After dinner looking through the family photograph albums with her, while the others played poker which he did not play — gambling made him nervous — and Mr Lumley wound the grandfather clock. Going up to bed alone and feeling twinges of self-pity as he lay in the darkness hearing the raucous cries of the poker players coming from downstairs. Drifting asleep and being woken as Jennifer, who had crept from her room, dropped her nightdress and climbed in beside him, complaining that Bertie had cheated at cards. Smiling as she pulled at his pyjama bottoms while chiding him for being dressed. As for the Saturday, it was claustrophobic, with the wet making it difficult to get out, with too much to eat at breakfast and too much talk about eating and drinking, and something going on between Hilary and Henderson which he wasn't being allowed to know about, an exclusion he resented. And, as he mused when he'd finished remembering, he wasn't even halfway through the Saturday and still Sunday to go . . . .

Clack, clack, clack. The glasses went onto the tray, with a sound like stones rolling on a greenhouse roof.

What would Mrs Lumley make of herself? he wondered, if she could have seen herself at that moment. Nothing probably. Mrs Lumley never thought she was rude or ill-tempered. Mrs Lumley, he realised, always thought of herself as exquisitely well-mannered.

'These glasses have been with us in the family for over a hundred years,' Fergus heard her saying. He turned to look at her. 'Do you think you can manage without breaking them?'

'No, I think you'd better carry them for me,' he said jokily.

Mrs Lumley opened her rather small eyes. 'Don't be so wet,' she said.

'It's a joke, mother,' called Hilary from the corner.

He went around the table and picked up the tray. The glasses were thin with a filigree design around the rims. Mrs Lumley was fussing with the catch of the cabinet even though he'd closed it firmly. Carrying the tray he took two steps forward, stopped and stood stoically in front of the door from the kitchen. He was waiting for her to open it. After a few seconds it became clear. No, it wasn't going to happen, which was one up for him.

He was about to turn so he could put down the tray and do it for himself. At this point Mrs Lumley lunged forward.

'I'll do it,' she said ferociously.

She wrenched on the handle with enormous force. Now the edge of the door was hurtling towards him and he realised he was standing too close.

The next few moments were in slow motion. The corner of the door hit the edge of the tray. It tilted violently. The glasses slid like skittles across the shiny surface and then jumped over the lip. A second later he heard them tinkling onto the flagged floor making a surprisingly delicate and undramatic noise.

He braced himself. Mrs Lumley's eyes clouded with tears. She covered her face with her hands, and let out a cry of rage. Her whole body heaved and wobbled in pain like a shaking jelly.

'I'm terribly sorry,' said Fergus firmly. 'Can you tell me where the dustpan and brush is?' The desire to laugh had taken him with a vengeance and he was biting the inside of his cheeks.

The hands came away from her face and two dark eyes stared at him. You're a past master at this, aren't you? he thought.

'Weren't you looking where you were going?' said Mrs Lumley. 'Isn't it perfectly obvious that if a door opens out you stand well back from it?'

The offending door opened and Jim Lumley crunched in with an apologetic look, asking what had happened. He was a husband with a sixth sense where his wife's furies were concerned.

'Don't stand on it, you idiot, it's broken glass,' Mrs Lumley shouted, pointing at the ground.

'It's all right, Kay,' he said, 'I'll sweep it up.'

'It's all right? All right?' she screamed at the top of her voice. The high point of the performance was coming. 'The engagement's off and you'd better have a long talk to that Henderson,' she screamed, 'and Clive's got to be told.'

Fergus looked down. The story was out.

Pieces of glass glistened around Mr Lumley's polished brogues. The door banged shut and he heard Mrs Lumley sobbing as she ran along the corridor outside.

At lunch Jim apologised for his wife's absence, explaining she had a headache. That afternoon he took Henderson for a long walk.

34

They were playing the Truth Game in the living room now the Lumley parents had gone to bed. Hilary had confessed to stealing from Biba's, while Henderson had admitted to lying to a prospective buyer in order to raise their offer on a painting. Now it was Jennifer's go with the question. What was your greatest act of betrayal to which you've never confessed?

She was standing with her back to the fire, clumsily holding a cigarette and tugging on the string of pearls around her neck. Watching her closely, Fergus felt his affections stirring. She was nervous. He would have liked to put his arms around her. His thoughts drifted to the end of the evening, when she would steal to his bedroom as she had the evening before and climb in beside him. He would tell her then what he had felt whilst she had stood against the fireplace covered with invitations. He would tell her then as he kissed her on the eyelids, and she would nuzzle him in response and tug at his pyjama cord. The fact was, over the months they'd grown fond of each other. They were now a little in love with each other, he realised. They'd even talked about living together.

'Well,' Jennifer swallowed and rolled her lips.

'Note the simulated nervousness, everyone,' shouted Hilary. 'One whopper coming up.'

'My greatest act of betrayal . . .' Jennifer stopped and looked down at the carpet.

'. . . Was . . . oh, I can't, I can't, I can't.'

'Come on, Jennifer,' coaxed Henderson, 'get it out. You'll feel better when you do.'

'. . . was the police. No I won't.'

At her words Fergus sensed his adrenalin trickling. He stared at her face but it was cast down. It was not possible, he told himself, but the thought was lodged and nothing that was thought could ever be unthought.

'The police,' said Henderson, who felt he had made a serious admission and wanted someone else to make one equal to his, 'what about them?'

Jennifer looked up. Her whole face was suffused red.

'No, I won't, I won't, I won't,' she said.

Jennifer ran back to her place on the sofa opposite him and sat down with her legs tucked underneath. Keeping her head lowered, she took a strand of hair and began to examine the ends.

'Jennifer loses a life,' said Hilary, 'and now I want to go out again so you can get something really meaty out of me.' She playfully knocked her shoulder against Fergus beside her. 'Let's not get too serious,' she said. 'It's only a game, after all.'

She ran from the room.

They started to discuss what question to put to Hilary in quiet, low tones but Fergus paid no attention. He looked across the room. Jennifer sat, a small, still figure, alone on the end of a sofa.

35

Fergus lay up in his bed, leaning against the headrest. Beyond the uncurtained windows stretched a blue-black sky and the darkened Leicestershire countryside.

Jennifer came in. He heard her nightdress slipping off and falling to the floor. She climbed in beside him.

'You're not very friendly,' said Jennifer.

'I don't feel very friendly.'

A door banged and Yummy barked once.

'They had a horrible policewoman,' Jennifer began, 'with a torch. She said she was going to strip me naked and stare up my bum. I told them everything.'

She was lying on her back, staring straight up at the ceiling. She reminded him of a statue on a sepulchre.

'You should have told me,' he said.

In his thoughts, he was in the conservatory at the party, looking down at the communal garden, watching the man and his dog pacing the glimmering gravel pathway. Hilary was leaning against the balustrade. They started to talk. Someone touched him. It was Jennifer with a carnival hat on the side of her head. She led him away. 'You looked as though you needed rescuing,' she said.

They left the party. The hostess, Mrs Dixon, was at the conservatory window and overheard Jennifer's imitation. They ran along the pavement. They had been strangers at the start of the evening but now they were partners in mischief.

They trailed up the stairs to her flat, laughing. Fergus felt excitement mounting as the moment drew closer and closer when they would climb into bed. They stepped over the threshold, laughing. Her expression changed and she disappeared into the lavatory for ten minutes, leaving him in the living room under the white lampshade. Clive appeared in his absurd scarf and fell asleep with his mouth open.

She showed him her bedroom. He climbed into her four-poster. The pillow smelt of shampoo. She appeared and they talked about Thumper. She climbed in beside him. They kissed and caressed. She made love to him. Afterwards, they fell asleep.

That was three or four or at the most five hours after the police station, three or four or at the most five hours after Jennifer's telling them what had happened in the restaurant. The statement which he had seen in Curry's file was surely hers.

'Why don't you answer me?' he said. He was thinking about the maroon Vauxhall sitting outside his flat. It hadn't been his imagination and now he had a good idea where it came from. It was from Curry, waiting for the lead.

'There's no should about it,' said Jennifer, echoing what he'd said what felt like minutes before. 'And since we're still playing the Truth Game, I should tell you that a little bird told me that you've been fucking Laura again.'

Yes, it was true. The thought was cold and clinical. After the evening in the restaurant and again in the New Year when he came back from Dublin they'd spent the night together. But compared to the issue in question it was insignificant, he told himself. He decided to say nothing.

They sat in silence. His shoulders grew cold. There was an owl hooting in a tree.

He reached for a saucer and put it between them. He handed her a cigarette and took one for himself. He lit hers and then his.

They smoked in the darkness. When they were finished the stubs were put out, leaving an after-smell of burnt paper. The saucer was put away again. Fergus wriggled down into bed. Jennifer caressed him through his pyjamas. Without his taking them off they made love mechanically.

When Fergus woke up in the morning, the space beside him was empty.

36

It was getting dark when the Dyane pulled up in Natal Street on Sunday evening. Fergus took his bag out of the boot and slammed the lid shut.

'I'll be seeing you then,' said Henderson.

A fine damp drizzle hung in the air.

Henderson nodded towards the dark head of Jennifer in the back.

'Women,' he said, raising his eyes upwards.

Throughout that Sunday she hadn't spoken to Fergus once.

'When they are nice, they are very very nice, but when they are bad they are horrid.'

He shook hands with Fergus. The Dyane puttered off. Henderson put his arm out of the window and waved back. After the car disappeared from sight Fergus stood on the pavement. His flat would be cold after standing empty for two days. Perhaps he would ring Laura? Then he remembered she was busy.

Fergus went inside and unpacked. Then he went into the front room and stared out of the window. In the laundrette Mrs Walsh was mopping the floor. He could just make out long trails of white suds on the linoleum.

He opened his cigarette packet. It was empty. He pulled out the sleeve of silver-covered paper and crumpled up the cardboard. A fire engine sailed by, its bulk appearing to take up the entire width of the road.

He found his coat and pulled it on. He felt oddly nervous. When he went outside he carefully double-locked the door.

The evening was cold. He noticed a faint hoar-breath as he slipped down the stairs and that his footfalls had a curious dead sound.

On the halfway landing he found himself reaching into his pocket for his keys even though he knew he'd put them there a couple of moments before, and then checking for his wallet. Damn that nagging feeling, he thought. It reminded him of the itch that had plagued him when his arm had been in plaster. He had poked at it for hours with a knitting needle to absolutely no avail. But when the cast came off, of course the itch disappeared.

He paused outside the Singhs' front door. Not a sound came from inside. He went down the path in the direction of the pavement and looked back. The curtains in the front room were tightly closed but lights behind were on.

He crossed the road and went into the Kwik-Mart. It was brightly lit with neon. The woman in the sari by the cash till sat with her head resting on her hand. A programme of Indian music played on the radio. The noise was distorted and tinny. He saw a rack of brightly coloured greetings cards with a two-foot one in the middle, embossed with a huge silver key and the message *'Happy 21st'*.

He made his way past shelves crowded with tins of Bolognese sauce and Brasso to the far corner. Tarpaulins lay rolled on the filthy floor. At nine o'clock they would be used to cover over the alcohol. He took a half-bottle of Highland Cream from the shelf because it was the cheapest whisky and went back to the front.

'Anything else?' asked the woman, lazily punching the till. Her fingernails were streaked with old varnish. She had a blue-coloured stone on an earring in the side of her nose.

Fergus pointed towards his brand of cigarettes and asked for twenty.

The woman took the money and gave him his change. The tray shut and his receipt fluttered to the floor, where there were others grubby from where she had trodden them down.

Outside the street was empty. He could hear the sitar music through the glass shop front.

He started to walk and thought he heard something behind. He turned. There was nothing. He looked from the Kwik-Mart to the darkened interior of the fish and chip shop and then to the laundrette. Mrs Walsh was smoking a cigarette. Her mop was leaning against the window at an unruly angle.

He slipped the bottle of whisky into the pocket of his coat. With its thin kidney shape it fitted snugly.

He stepped down from the kerb and began to cross the road. Something was behind again. He stopped. It stopped. His mouth felt dry.

He started to run. With half a dozen paces he was across the road and onto the pavement on the other side. He could see the path to his block stretching ahead with muddy patches of grass on either side, and the stairs lit with a single lightbulb at the end.

His feet found the bottom tread, his hand the metal railing. He pulled himself up. His footfalls were like small explosions. He was smarting between his lungs. He reached the halfway landing. The graffiti on the shiny brick walls flashed by: 'QPR for ever' and 'I love Maureen'. The first floor was in view. His hand went into his pocket, fumbled past the packet of cigarettes and found his keys. He drew them out. He jumped up the last three steps. He separated the long key to the deadlock and inserted it. The mechanism inside clicked. He was aware of a sudden silence. Nothing was moving. Nothing was near him. He turned around. The stairway was empty. The balcony in each direction was empty. Beyond the parapet shone the street lamps. His heart was thumping. It was the only noise in the hush.

He opened the door and went in. The latch clicked behind him. He leaned against the wood. There was sweat on his forehead. He could feel his heart slowly returning to its regular pattern.

Pouf! The hall lightbulb exploded, showering him with glass. The dryness in his mouth returned and his muscles felt watery.

37

He picked his way over the glass and went down the corridor. He hung his coat on the back of a chair and found the dustpan and brush.

'All right,' he said, retracing his steps, 'that's quite enough, Fred, for one night. No more lightbulbs. Go to sleep.'

His voice echoed back to him through the empty flat.

He began to sweep, the bristles scratching on the linoleum. It was hard to see where all the splinters were because he only had the light of the living room to go by. He ended up sweeping everywhere.

When he was finished the pile of dust and glass went into the pan. He returned to the kitchen and pressed the pedal of the bin. His sweepings clattered down onto the empty tin of lychees in the bottom, almost hidden amongst the folds of plastic. His foot came off the pedal. He turned. Stopped. Turned back. Pressed. The lid lifted off. He looked down. The lychee can lay there covered with dirt and dusty pieces of glass. He picked it up by the lid, sharp serrations around the edges which pricked his skin. He walked to the sink. The can went under the cold tap. The rushing water washed it clean. He put it on the drainer. He looked at it. Surely he had to be dreaming?

Check first, he told himself. He opened the fridge. There was butter, Anchor, half a pound. There was milk, carton unopened. There was a lemon. There was a jar of red cabbage. There was the pack of vodka miniatures, minus one. And there was where the can of lychees had lived. He shut the door. He went back to the sink. He looked at the tin. He remembered Ravi coming to the door with it. Noticing the price, the green spots of age on the metal. He hadn't eaten them. Or had he? Could he recall opening them? Can openers were such a struggle one didn't forget that. Or eating them. Cold orbs that tasted sweet. Almost like eyes but not eyes because, inside from where the smooth stone was taken, there were rough callouses and ridges. Nothing eye-like about that. Always a surprise after the clean smooth flesh. Was it an experience he could remember having? It wasn't an experience he'd had recently. Recently? Absolutely not.

He ran into the front room and opened the doors of the sideboard. On the velvet-covered shelves lay the collection of cranberry-coloured glasses. He could smell the oil in the hinges. He stared into the dark corners. Nothing. He went to the sofa and pulled it from the wall. The top of the skirting board was covered with a layer of grey fluff. He picked up a couple of twopenny pieces from the floor. Two clean rounds were left behind in the dust.

In the hallway he peeped behind the canvases with his bicycle light, pointing with the beam into the triangle of darkness. Again, nothing. He went into the bathroom and climbed onto the edge of the bath. On top of the medicine cabinet he found two packets of razor blades and old tubes of ointment with the paint flaking from them. That was all. He climbed down and saw his shoes had left a black mark on the edge. As he wiped it off he wondered, was it wise to give way to anxiety? But once given way to, he couldn't change his mind.

He went into the kitchen and opened every cupboard and pulled out every drawer. He also peered into the oven and behind the refrigerator. The exertion involved in searching the flat made him feel warm. He could feel his panic subsiding.

He left the kitchen and went into his bedroom. As he clicked on the light he rejoiced he did not sleep in a bed but on a mattress that rested firmly on the floor.

The cupboard door creaked as he pulled it back. His clothes hung from the rail in a neat row. He clambered up on the wicker chair and surveyed the top, strewn with Kenny Ogden's old paintbrushes and oil paints.

Nothing.

Fergus went into the kitchen and poured himself a tumbler of whisky. He went into the front room. He pulled over a chair to put his feet on, and sat down on the sofa. Leaning back, some tiny thing wasn't right. The cushion was plumper than he remembered.

He let his arm lie along the crease between the seat and the armrest. As he drank he stroked his finger up and down. Perhaps there was something there? Box of matches. Mascara sticks. Paperback books. He dug down. There was something. It felt shiny, like polythene. He put his glass on the shelf and turned to the side. His hand went in. He scissored with his fingers around a corner. He tugged. He could see an edge sticking out. He took hold of it with his other hand and pulled. It came away effortlessly. Out in the light he saw it was a cellophane packet with a reddish vein along the top which sealed it airtight. Inside there were tiny hand-made envelopes about an inch and a half long. He took one out and opened it carefully. Inside there was a flattened oblong of pinkish powder. It was a one-gram deal, just like those he had enjoyed the spring before. With the other six like it, that made a quarter of an ounce. 'You've been a very good boy.' Curry's words returned to him. With this in his possession he'd be the opposite. Having failed as a lead he'd reverted to his original fate. He ran to the bathroom and flushed it all away and then for good measure flushed half a dozen times afterwards.

133

38

At half past eleven, four hours after Henderson had dropped him back, the police arrived: five in uniform, one a handler with a dog; and two in plain clothes.

Fergus sat in the kitchen under the watchful eye of a young constable while they searched the flat. On his forehead perspiration glowed and Fergus wiped it away with a tea towel.

'Would you like a cup of tea?' he asked and the constable shook his head.

He could hear the noise of the dog's paws on the linoleum and drawers being opened and shut.

Somehow, at some time, he thought, he must have done a good deed, for now the eyes had rewarded him with his discovery in the sofa and he was going to escape.

'Constable French,' shouted a voice, 'come on.'

The policeman picked his helmet off the table and went into the hall.

The sound of a hinge creaking and feet tramping and then of his own front door shutting came to Fergus.

'Hello,' he called and realised they had gone and he was alone.

39

Fergus walked away from Berwick Street market carrying a small bunch of yellow daffodils. The tissue paper around them was sodden where it touched their stems.

'You haven't replied to my letters, old man,' said Mr Wiggins coming up behind him. 'Very pretty daffodils. Were they expensive?' he added slyly.

He was in his brown suit and carried his plastic attaché case. On his head he was wearing a red-and-white-striped woollen hat with a bobble on the end. He looked ridiculous.

'I have not replied to your letters,' Fergus heard himself shouting, 'and I will not be replying to your letters in the future, either. Goodbye, Mr Wiggins.'

He pushed the flowers into the older man's free hand and hurried away without looking back.

At half past three, when Martin-Smith was complaining on the telephone that after two years his chair was still not mended, the runner delivered a letter to Fergus with his name printed on the front. The handwriting was unfamiliar. As he tore it open a rubbery smell escaped. Then he saw that inside there was a prophylactic, neatly knotted, its reservoir well filled. He dropped the insult and its envelope straight into a Jiffy bag and summoned Melanie.

'Have this burnt,' he said, handing her the package.

40

It was Saturday, six days after the visit by the police. Fergus went to the museums in Exhibition Road, returning home in the early evening.

He walked along the pavement towards his block. Two children holding either end of a piece of string were shuffling along the pavement.

Skirting the low wall which fenced off the grass, he thought he detected the curtain moving in the front room of the Singhs' flat. As he passed the front door, it opened and Mr Singh's bloodshot eyes peered out.

'Fergus,' he called, and handed him a piece of paper. The

message on it was made up with letters which had been cut out from newspapers and magazines. It was like an old-fashioned blackmail note. It read: *Get out or you're dead. This is your last warning.*

Fergus looked from the paper to Mr Singh. His skin seemed to have been drawn back tightly over his small square face. His breath was sweet but mixed with alcohol.

'I'm ready for the bastards, I'll kill them if I have to defend my home, my family,' he said.

From the kitchen behind, Mrs Singh said something. She was sitting at the table with Mira. Mr Singh turned round and spoke back loudly to them. Fergus read the message again:

Get out or you're dead. This is your last warning.

41

On the pavement a few shoppers straggled home with their bags. There was a peculiar atmosphere in the street of expectancy, even excitement, which only came early on Saturday nights.

The police station lay ahead, a grey building with steps. Why exactly was he going there? Fergus wondered. Because it was the right thing to do, he told himself. But why couldn't Mr Singh or his wife have gone? They had both irritated him when he had been at their front door. Mr Singh because of his drunken bravura and Mrs Singh because of her churlishness. Why had she just sat at the table and barked in Hindi? When he had proposed going on their behalf to the station, why hadn't she said something? A word of thanks. There was something lumpy and ungracious about her manner which he resented and he didn't like the way they both seemed to take for granted he would run around for them.

He was almost at the steps. He stopped and looked at the board with its 'Have You Seen?' posters. All the way there he'd been expecting to feel apprehensive. Flutters in the stomach. Adrenalin in the system. An increase in the rate of his heartbeat. But nothing. It was as if the Sunday evening before had never happened. It had been the same after his father's death. For weeks he'd been incredulous, unable to believe, and several times he'd caught himself thinking, planning, speculating as if his father were alive. This was the same; and he knew it would be a while before he could accept what had happened and not until then would he be able to feel frightened or angry.

42

He was in a small, low room with a counter running across the middle. On the grey walls there were posters advising the public to 'Lock out thieves' and others giving a twenty-four-hour telephone number which could be used to report drug-dealers.

The policeman behind the counter looked up. 'What can I do for you?' he asked.

Fergus handed across the note. The policeman looked at it carefully.

'The family who live underneath me are Asians. They received this recently,' said Fergus.

'When was that, sir?'

'I don't know. This morning, or last night.'

He was annoyed at not being able to answer the question.

'How did you come by this, sir?'

The policeman had a pink, flushed face and white hair. He was about thirty years old.

'As I was coming home this evening they showed it to me,' said Fergus.

The policeman made a note of the relevant names and addresses. When he finished he said, 'You'll have to get one of them to come down and make a report.'

137

A man in a suit, overweight, who looked like a detective appeared behind the counter. Glancing at Fergus he opened the drawer of a filing cabinet.

'They can't come down.'

'Why not?'

'They're frightened.'

The detective looked over his shoulder in a pointed manner. Fergus wondered if he was talking too loudly.

'Look. I don't know for certain there is a Singh family or that they've received this,' said the policeman politely.

He wrote something down on a pad and tore off the top sheet.

'This is our number,' he said. 'They can ring us to tell us what's been happening, or if there's any further trouble. And I'll send someone down to see them.'

'When?'

'Sometime in the next few days.'

Fergus said goodbye and went into the street. A high-pitched tone was coming from a nearby pedestrian crossing although no one was using it. A furniture store announced a 'Monster Suicide Closing Down Sale' in huge red letters. Two freckled boys were dragging a huge sheepdog along on a piece of rope. The animal put its front legs out straight and sank onto its haunches.

'Come on,' shouted the boys.

They heaved and the toenails of the dog scraped on the pavement like a metal spoon on a metal pan.

Fergus headed back in the direction of home.

43

Mr Singh stood in his doorway.

'You have to make a report in person,' Fergus said.

Mr Singh took the threatening note which Fergus was holding out.

'I can't go,' he said.

'Why not?'

'Special reason. My own reason.'

'I'm sorry I didn't have more luck at the station,' apologised
Fergus.

Mr Singh raised his hand, signalling that it was goodbye.

'Bang on the ceiling if you should want me,' said Fergus
hurriedly.

He pointed in the air.

Mr Singh nodded and closed the door.

44

Later that evening, the doorbell pealed. Through the frosted
glass Fergus could just make out a dark outline.

He opened the door and took half a step back. The caller's face
was painted white with blood-red lips.

'I'm terribly sorry to trouble you,' said the man, 'I'm going to a
fancy dress in case you're wondering why I'm dressed like this.'

The man removed the black top hat from his head. His long
and unruly hair compromised the effect, which was reassuring.

'I'm trying to find Flat 38, Durban House.'

'This is Flat 12, as you can see from the number on the door,'
Fergus said tetchily, 'and this is Mafeking House. Durban is the
next block along and you'll find 38 on the third floor, probably.'

The man followed Fergus across the balcony, his red-lined
cape floating behind.

Fergus said, 'That's Durban,' and pointed. He could hear
music and the faint sound of laughter across the darkness.

'I really am sorry I gave you a fright just now,' apologised the
man. 'I suppose the moral of the story is, don't travel around as
Count Dracula. I came by tube. The comments were unbeliev-
able. Stop for a bite at McDonalds. You never know when the

139

nibbles will strike. Worst was this young girl, I don't know, eight or nine years old. Burst into tears at the sight of me. Her mother had to take her into the next carriage.'

'It was murder but you loved it.'

Count Dracula smiled and replied, 'I suppose I did.'

He put his hat on his head and tapped it elegantly with a white gloved hand.

'Goodbye,' he said and disappeared down the stairs, whistling 'It's a Long Way to Tipperary'.

Fergus stayed on the balcony, the noise of the party was quite audible. He tried to imagine what it might be like. There'd be someone as Jesus in sandals and a smock made from a white sheet. The South American was another favourite, requiring only a big hat, a blanket slung over the shoulder as a poncho, and a large burnt cork moustache. There'd be some Marilyn Monroes of course, in clinging gowns and elbow-length gloves, and no fancy dress event was ever complete without a schoolboy in cap and short trousers, with a catapult sticking out of the back pocket.

Count Dracula waved from below and Fergus turned towards his door.

45

Asleep in bed Fergus began to dream vividly of an old walled town, his father, improbably dressed in a cowboy hat, and a Frankenstein-like monster who impaled himself on a thorn bush.

After some hours, Fergus opened his eyes. He could smell something. He clicked on the lamp. There was something squeezing itself through the cracks in the floorboards. It was some moments before he recognised it was smoke.

He scrambled into his clothes and ran into the hallway. There was smoke everywhere, as if a fog had invaded. Billowing in the air, it registered with him as oddly beautiful.

The smoke began to hurt his eyes. He ran outside onto the balcony and saw the street lamps. He wondered what time it was and remembered he had left his watch by his bed.

He hoisted his jumper up over his nose and ran back inside. The smoke was already thicker. He dragged Kenny's canvases outside and leant them against the parapet. In the distance he noticed the noise of a party, the guests chattering and the thump of music.

He went back inside again and stumbled through the living room. The furnishings were dark shapes. He reached around the side of the sofa and felt it, smooth and plastic. His hands found the thin, square handles of the tool box. He picked it up and ran out.

Down by the Singhs' he heard people running in the darkness. He saw a woman in an apron, a white hat and the black dress of a caricature maid, followed by an angel with trembling wings, his surplice lifted to reveal sandals and bare legs. They shouted something about going to ring the fire brigade.

Fergus smashed away the slats and pulled out the glass. His hand went through as smoke funnelled out. One chain, two chains, three chains fell away. The mortice clicked. The party-goers were cheering him on from the walkway of Durban House.

He took two, three, four, five steps forward. He was in a dark world without any bearings. His lungs were paining. He went along what he thought was a corridor and through a door. Was that something? It looked like a figure lying on a bed. If he could get to it, he could pull it out. But his legs were folding. He was sliding down the wall. His knees were hitting the ground. He was on the floor. The thought crossed his mind slowly, he had not made himself go there. He screwed up his eyes. He had to go on. But his body was turning. He wanted one thing but it was doing something else. A will of its own. The door he had come through was in front of him, a lighter dark to the dark of the wall. No, he wanted to turn back. His hand moved forward, his knee following. He was back in the passage. He would go out and breathe, fill his lungs with the cold night air. Then he would come back. Yes, out to the cool, the clean air. But which way was that? Now all was darkness. He was hurting everywhere. His hands were still moving, his knees following. There was an oblong shape with light behind it. Closer and closer it was coming. He felt the fuzziness of the mat and then something cold. He was sinking forward. There was something slithery on his cheek. His throat was raw, tasting of smoke as he coughed and spewed. There was a sound of running. Yes. It was coming towards him. Closer and closer. Tapering, high heel. Sandal flapping. Someone pulling. Yes. Pulling. Body inert, a huge sack filled with charcoal. Yes. Everything beginning to fade, the feeling like sliding. Yes. Fading, fading out . . . .

Fergus could feel himself coming to. His neck was hurting and his cheek was wet. He opened his eyes. The concrete smelt vaguely of leaf and damp. 'Are you all right?' He turned his head. It was the angel. His wings were silver. The woman was beside him. She held out a hand. 'Can you stand up?' she said. A red garter circled the top of her stocking. Two ambulances had come. And fire engines. Swathes of purple washed across the brick-work. Someone shouted to turn off the bloody sirens. The firemen in glistening overalls unfurled their hoses. A metal T was stuck into the ground and turned. The water began to flow, spray-ing everywhere. 'Stand back, please.' Blossom-white plastic tapes sealed off the area. A crowd watched with eyes glowing red. Blue-coated policemen whispered into their lapels. Bump, bump, bump. The wheels of the stretchers clattered and turned. Then, a few minutes later, one, two, three of them. Dark shapes under the blankets. One long, two short. The ambulance men were hurry-ing, obscenely hasty. Heads turned and stared. Up and in went the blanketed biers. The doors closed. Mr Singh was wailing. The sirens came on again and purple splashing everywhere. Mira sat on a wall weeping and weeping. 'Give them a cup of tea,' someone said. 'Take them away . . .' said someone else. The angel wore a crown of tinsel around his head. The maid shivered, stamping her heels.

'You went in and then you crawled out,' she said.

'Bloody funny giving you artificial respiration with these,' said the angel. He waved his wings.

A fireman splashed about in a huge puddle of dirty water. Men in white coats hammered plywood over the scorched windows. There had been three blanket biers, he remembered. He gave his details to a detective: name, address, place of work. No, he was free to go. A fireman helped him drag Kenny's canvases inside. He got a lift in a police car to the Uxbridge Road and found a taxi

to take him to Bayswater. Yawning, Laura opened the door.
'Look what the cat brought in,' she said. Five minutes later he was
snoring on the sofa, the tea she had made him steaming on the
chair.

46

The coffins were black and the screws along the top were brass,
shining like newly minted coins. From the back of the crematorium chapel Fergus stared across the heads and shoulders of the
mourners. There were three coffins: one for Mrs Singh, one for
Ravi and one for his brother. It was the first time Fergus had ever
seen children's coffins and to his eye they didn't seem to have the
same swelling and tapering proportions as the large one. They
were more box-like and somehow seemed to beckon, like a chest,
to be opened.

A button was pressed. A motor started up and the rollers of the
conveyor belt began to turn. Not unlike a factory, Fergus thought
in a vague way. As they moved forward the coffins rose and fell
gently, like boats making their way at sea.

The hole into which the conveyor belt fed was covered with a
dark silky-looking cloth. The head of the first coffin which was
Mrs Singh's now began to nose through and the cloth lifted as it
pushed forward into whatever lay behind. Her husband let out a
heart-rending cry from the front. The thirty or so mourners
around him, all friends or relatives of the family, responded with
a nervous shuffling of feet. Two cousins each took an arm and
supported Mr Singh's square, short body.

The coffin was halfway through the hole, the drape streaming
overhead and darkness showing on either side. Fergus peered,
half-expecting to see hands reaching out, but there were none.
Yet somewhere behind they were waiting, and he imagined dirty
aprons and calloused palms and the stale smell of Woodbine. He

heard a distant clock chiming and counted four. Four o'clock. It was tea-time and in factories and offices and kitchens pots were brewing, cups were steaming, spoons were scooping into bowls of sugar, and there was the smell of milk mingled with tannin. The men behind would very likely have a kettle on too. For some reason he imagined it would have a bakelite handle, broken and mended with sellotape.

Mrs Singh's coffin was through the hole. The covering dropped. Then the coffin of one of the boys started to nose its way in. The foot shuffling had stopped and a rapt state of attention spread through the mourners. The callous thump of the rollers and the noise of the motor were more audible now and, it seemed to Fergus, more oppressive. Why couldn't they have managed supreme silence? he wondered. But it was a stupid question to have asked. Once again, he returned to the word that summed up everything from beginning to end — thoughtlessness. In his whole life, this, it had suddenly seemed obvious to him, had been the common quality. It was a charge he could accuse others of too, he recognised that. But Fergus felt disinclined to point the finger. That would have dodged the issue. He had to take responsibility himself. Not only could he not let others shoulder his responsibility but, as he had been reminding himself, there was nothing other than his own self over which he had any influence.

The drape dropped as the second coffin disappeared and then looped up again as the third began to make its way through. Fergus let his gaze drift to the corner where there were flowers in a jug, yellow blooms which seemed especially bright against the grey walls, and then upwards to the inscription in Latin which ran just under the ceiling and which he was too tired to even try to translate.

He let his glance drop just as the drape was about to fall for the third and final time. He watched it closely, the coffin underneath gliding forward and it swishing down. Suddenly he felt a short tremor of pain passing through him. The fall of the material said the same as the hollow sound of earth on the coffin lid. It said that he couldn't go on imagining the sound of the boys playing on the stairs, or the tapes of trembling sitar music which sometimes had drifted up through the floor in the evening, or the cooking smells which had lingered in the passageway. He had been conjuring these up since the night of the fire, during the long evenings when he had sat in his scorched-smelling flat. But now some irrevoc-able point had been passed, and he would have to face it. Mrs Singh and the boys were gone.

The double doors at the side of the chapel were opened by a crematorium official dressed in a dark suit. Everyone filed out-side and Fergus was aware of the next set of mourners already jostling at the front of the building. There was a wind blowing and it flapped the women's saris hanging down below the hems of raincoats. The men, they were in suits and coats, buttoned themselves up. A few spots of rain fell. The ashes had to be waited for and so everyone sheltered under an arch. Someone had brought a folding stool for Mr Singh and he sat on it, hold-ing his head in his hands and rocking backwards and forwards.

Fergus was introduced to Mrs Singh's brother, a man with a coconut-shaped head and purplish lips. They talked about Mira and Fergus learnt she had come to England on holiday and de-cided not to return to India. She had survived the fire, but then the Home Office had deported her, not even allowing her to stay for the funeral. Fergus wondered if she was the special reason Mr Singh wouldn't go to the police.

'I would think so,' agreed the brother.

He had the same chihuahua-like eyes as his sister. He began to describe his journey from Yorkshire, where he lived, to London. The bus was cheaper than the train and so much more comfortable. Fergus nodded, staring from the arch where he stood back into the Garden of Remembrance which stretched behind. Flags of York stone enclosed beds of earth with dull green rose bushes growing in them which trembled in the wind. Near a melancholy yew tree a woman scrubbed a metal vase with a Brillo pad, a sound which he could hear surprisingly well. She was crying quietly and one might even have thought con-tentedly as she went about her work. 'They showed a video,' he heard the brother saying — he was still describing his journey — and Fergus recognised it as one of those moments he knew he would never forget.

47

At that time of evening with the light not gone yet the street lamps showing, the stucco house fronts seemed to glimmer. They were almost ghostly. He was walking past a crescent-shaped garden and stopped to peer into it. On the branch ends of the bushes immediately in front he could just make out the candle shapes of little buds. Spring always filled him with the oddest emotion; a mingling of optimism and self-reproach. Anything was possible. On the other hand he was heavy with the sense of how he had wasted his time.

He sniffed the air smelling of earth and mould. The bitter-sweet feeling grew stronger. He should feel grateful for the sensation, he thought — such strong emotions didn't come often — yet to whom? He thought of the eyes in the sky. But one was hardly grateful to the eyes, he decided. Silent watchers, what did they have to do with it? April came every twelve months and with April came the feeling. It wasn't a gift. It was a consequence.

Clack, clack, clack sounded a toy gun. Two young boys playing at war were chasing each other across the grass. Fergus looked at his watch. He had better hurry, he told himself, if he was going to get to Laura's dinner. He walked away, imagining the mixed feeling of joy and reproach lying in the middle of his body like a second heart.

He crossed over the Fulham Road and went into the redbrick mansion block where Laura's father and stepmother lived. The smell of polish lingering in the foyer, from which once he had drawn such reassurance, now he noticed simply with pleasure. Looking to the future, there was less dependence on the past.

The tiny lift carried him upwards, light slanting through the grille doors as he passed each floor. On the lift wall there was a constantly changing pattern of shadow. On the fifth floor he climbed out and found the front door of the Shellgate flat was open. He took the present out of his pocket and hurried inside. As he pulled off his coat he heard Henderson saying loudly in the

146

living room, 'What happened when Tarzan jumped onto the window ledge with her?'

'Why, she burst into tears of course and shrieked "Don't drop me. I'm terrified of heights".' It was a moment or two before he recognised it was Jennifer speaking. But of course. She would have been invited too. Why had he assumed she wouldn't be? If he'd thought about it he'd have known she would.

The door of the living room opened. Laura's stepmother came out in a gypsy dress with a matching headband.

'Fergus, dear.'

He kissed her powdered cheek while glancing through the door to where the others were.

'How much did this revenge caper cost you, Jennifer?' called out Henderson.

Fergus entered the room. On pink armchairs and yellow sofas, heads and torsoes swivelled.

'Welcome, Fergus.' The figure of Mr Shellgate strode towards him in a smoking jacket and velvet slippers. The memory of the argument in the restaurant the night Laura had cried and his small residue of resentment were dispersed by the welcome.

'How nice of you to join us. What'll you have to drink?'

At the sideboard his elderly host poured pale champagne into a glass. It bubbled up and ran over the side.

'Jolly good luck to spill.' Philip Shellgate wiped the dark wood. 'Have you heard this story of Jennifer's?'

'Don't,' Jennifer cried, 'it's too humiliating.'

Fergus looked. She was sitting on the sofa with her back towards him, her legs tucked underneath, her hair trailing over one shoulder. That was the position he remembered her sitting in at the end of the Truth Game. Now, after months when they had not spoken, he was finding her sitting the same way again.

'Got one of those kissing gram people to come to the office,' said Philip Shellgate. 'Who was he?'

'Tarzan.'

'That's right. Part of a practical joke against the boss. He was meant to beat his chest and act as if he was going to jump from the window into the street. But it didn't work, did it?'

He stared at Jennifer, so she could finish.

'Thirty pounds,' cried Jennifer, 'plus VAT, it cost us in the office, to see Amanda crying in some big hulk's arms.'

Laura came up and Fergus gave her the present, a hardback edition of *The Catcher in the Rye*.

'Thank you,' she said, embracing him. 'I've something to show you.'

She took a typed letter from the sideboard.

'This is it. It's the best birthday present a girl could ask for. I've been showing it off all evening.'

It was a letter of confirmation from a publisher. Laura's history of art deco shopfronts had finally been commissioned.

Fergus went around the room. Alfred shook his hand limply. Jennifer kissed him quickly on the lips. Hetty stayed on the sofa, sunk low, so he had to bend down. Hilary offered her head with her eyes closed as if she half-expected a blow. Henderson twanged Fergus' braces and said, 'Hi.'

They went into the dining room where Mrs Shellgate had done all the stippling with her own hands. Everyone complimented her. On the dining table there were mother-of-pearl mats. Fergus dried the bottom of his champagne glass on his napkin leaving a wet circle. They ate smoked salmon, roast beef with small parsnips baked in brown sugar, and little new potatoes which Mrs Shellgate had bought especially in Harrods Food Hall that morning. Later the lights were dimmed and a cake the shape of a book brought in with candles on top. Everyone sang 'Happy Birthday', and Laura blew the candles out in one go. The portions were handed round and Fergus found a sixpence in his.

With coffee Mrs Shellgate produced a box of crackers and Fergus went round to Jennifer and said, 'You've been ignoring me all evening. Pull one with me.'

The cracker opened with a bang and the contents tumbled onto the floor. Jennifer instantly bent down to retrieve them.

'A policeman's whistle,' she said, handing him one that was green and plastic. In the mouth it tasted of bakelite.

'But it's yours. You won the cracker.' Fergus pointed to the length of cardboard and green tissue paper lying on her chair.

'And a red crown,' she said, shaking her head. She unfurled the paper hat and placed it on his head. 'You won it.'

Jennifer slid into her chair beside Hetty. Back in his own seat Fergus saw Jennifer wriggling and sensed words of reproach were being whispered. Hetty was telling her friend not to make such a show of herself. But as he knew, Hetty believed the way to a man's heart was to feign indifference.

Everyone was talking. Fergus stared at the wall with its stretched silk panels and stippled borders. He was thinking about the eyes. Once upon a time he'd imagined, not only did they look down on everything, but they also weighed in the balance, judged and meted out a retributory justice. But now, if he thought seriously about them, he imagined they were like barrage balloons, a decoy left to delude those below. There was no continuous assessment. There was no supervising intelligence balancing the actions of bad against good. There was no justice. There was only oneself making sense of what happened.

'Penny for your thoughts!' Jennifer called across the table.

'Oh, nothing.'

'That's a very nice new suit you're wearing.'

The doorbell rang. It was the first of those who'd been invited in after supper. Everyone went into the living room with its dusky red walls. Fergus sat down in an armchair. Charades were suggested and Mrs Shellgate began to tear up little pieces of scrap paper. A pair of hands slipped across Fergus' chest from behind and Jennifer put her head against his.

'I'm drunk,' she said. 'Have you forgiven me?'

He didn't know where to begin.

'I've nothing to forgive,' he said.

Jennifer squeezed him around the neck.

'Jennifer, leave Fergus alone and come and join your team,' someone shouted before he could reply.

Mr Shellgate began to run through the rules. Fergus looked up at the picture of the Oxford and Cambridge boat race hanging over the fireplace. There was only oneself making sense, he thought. In the past such an idea had frightened him. Now he saw it gave him hope because, with this sort of understanding, he was free to act. The heroin, of course, now he thought about it, had been perfectly suited to his old belief in the eyes. It replaced choice with appetite, which was no choice.

'Our team's to the hall,' ordered Laura.

He followed them out and stood at the edge of the huddle around the table. Henderson said he wanted to give Mrs Shellgate *Encyclopaedia Britannica*. Everyone laughed, Fergus as well. He could just imagine Ivy when her turn came, looking at her slip of paper, exclaiming in horror, putting it away, exclaiming again, fishing it out for a second look, then cursing while her team shouted, 'Come on, get on with it.' He was actually looking forward to the game.

48

Fergus and Jennifer left Laura's party together. At the Michelin building they turned south and made their way through dark, leafy streets to the King's Road. Opposite the barracks they stopped and looked up and down. There were no taxis with yellow *For Hire* signs to be seen.

'Let's walk,' said Fergus.

On the way from the Shellgates they had walked side by side but now she slipped an arm through his.

They started to move gently along the pavement.

'Miss me?' she asked.

He said that he did.

'I too,' she said.

They stopped before a brightly lit travel agent's with a poster in the window of a girl, and a rock, and a shimmering blue sea behind.

Jennifer repeated she was sorry. He squeezed her arm to show he understood.

They lapsed into silence as they stared at the window. There was only oneself making sense and he ought to make a start. Perhaps it was the letter which had finally propelled him into this way of thinking? It had arrived that morning: Dalkey postmark, Dalkey address, and inside the folded sheets of Basildon Bond notepaper covered in his mother's sloping writing. He could see it dancing before his eyes. 'Dearest Fergus,' it had begun:

. . . Pippa has been here. She left not long ago. She brought her boyfriend for the weekend. We had a nice time — or a nice enough time. This afternoon we went to Bray and climbed the head, just her and myself. I started to discuss our 'problem', saying we had to face facts and acknowledge the will her father left wasn't the one he really wanted. She had to share. I put it to her bluntly. I'd never intended to be so forthright. She *had* to share. Point blank she refused. We had a terrible argument. Passers-by who were out for a stroll stared at us. When we got back she packed and left. At that moment I realised that my prayers were never going to be answered. There are the courts of course but I don't think really either of us would want to do that. . . .

The image faded but the effect of the letter stayed with him, a mixture of anger and relief. No one liked to be dispossessed — and the letter was final confirmation that was his lot — but it was also a relief. Now he was free from his hopes. Now Pippa wouldn't have to lie any more. And now his mother wouldn't have to go on forcing herself to believe in what couldn't happen.

He saw his reflection in the glass and Jennifer's beside him. He looked at her face and her sticking-out ears, her brown mild eyes and her full generous lips. He felt a surge of warmth. Only oneself making sense and he had to start doing it. He knew now what the penalties would be if he didn't. Each time April came there'd be a little less hope and joy and a little more reproach and regret. The ambiguous feeling he'd felt looking into the garden earlier on would disappear and, in its place, would come a sense of defeat. Once that happened, life would be nothing more than an extended wait.

A taxi passed. Then in his mind's eye, he saw the two of them, Jennifer and himself, stretched out on a rock, the turquoise Mediterranean beside them, silver fish glinting in its depths, the sun beating down, warming and healing, and a clear blue sky arching above that was open unto space.

If Samuel Beckett had been born in Czechoslovakia we'd still be waiting for Godot

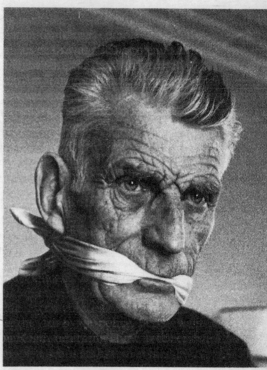

Samuel Beckett's "Waiting for Godot" is banned in Czechoslovakia.

In fact, any writing that differs from the opinions of the Czech government is banned in Czechoslovakia.

Luckily, Beckett does not live in Czechoslovakia, but what of those writers who do?

Fortunately, some of their work can be read in Index on Censorship, a magazine which fights censorship by publishing the work of censored poets, authors, playwrights, journalists and publishers.

We publish work from all over the world regardless of politics, religion or race.

Our contributions come from wherever work is censored.

We also publish commentaries, first-hand testimonials, factual reports and a country by country chronicle.

You'll always find publishers, writers and journalists at the front of the struggle for free speech.

Now you know where you can find their work.

Please write to us for a free copy of our magazine at: 39c Highbury Place London N5 1QP or you can telephone us on: 01-359 0161.

Index on Censorship for crying out loud.